APR 2 8 2005

Family for Keeps

*Also by Margaret Daley
in Large Print:*

What the Heart Knows

This Large Print Book carries the
Seal of Approval of N.A.V.H.

Family for Keeps

Margaret Daley

Thorndike Press • Waterville, Maine

Published in 2005 by arrangement with Harlequin Books S.A.

Thorndike Press® Large Print Christian Fiction.

The tree indicium is a trademark of Thorndike Press.

The text of this Large Print edition is unabridged.
Other aspects of the book may vary from the original edition.

Set in 16 pt. Plantin by Al Chase.

Printed in the United States on permanent paper.

Library of Congress Cataloging-in-Publication Data

Daley, Margaret.
  Family for keeps / by Margaret Daley.
    p. cm. — (Thorndike Press large print Christian fiction)
  ISBN 0-7862-7473-5 (lg. print : hc : alk. paper)
  1. Widowers — Fiction.   2. Single fathers — Fiction.
3. Football players — Fiction.   4. Nurses — Fiction.
5. Large type books.   I. Title.   II. Thorndike Press large
print Christian fiction series.
PS3604.A36F36 2005
813′.6—dc22   2004030434

I want to dedicate this book
to all the nurses and doctors,
especially my mother, Catherine,
and my goddaughter, Ruth.

As the Founder/CEO of NAVH, the only national health agency solely devoted to those who, although not totally blind, have an eye disease which could lead to serious visual impairment, I am pleased to recognize Thorndike Press★ as one of the leading publishers in the large print field.

Founded in 1954 in San Francisco to prepare large print textbooks for partially seeing children, NAVH became the pioneer and standard setting agency in the preparation of large type.

Today, those publishers who meet our standards carry the prestigious "Seal of Approval" indicating high quality large print. We are delighted that Thorndike Press is one of the publishers whose titles meet these standards. We are also pleased to recognize the significant contribution Thorndike Press is making in this important and growing field.

Lorraine H. Marchi, L.H.D.
Founder/CEO
NAVH

★ Thorndike Press encompasses the following imprints: Thorndike, Wheeler, Walker and Large Print Press.

For I the Lord thy God
will hold thy right hand,
saying unto thee,
Fear not; I will help thee.

— *Isaiah* 41:13

Chapter One

"Lady, it worries me when I see a clown cry."

Tess Morgan looked at the giant who was leaning in the doorway to the waiting room, his left leg, up to his knee, in a walking cast. She blinked, releasing the last few teardrops on her lashes. Absently she felt the tears cascade down her face as she tried to compose herself in front of an incredible-looking — hulk!

Oh, my, he's big. He filled the doorway with his immense frame, thick-muscled neck, broad shoulders and chest. That was her first impression of the stranger, but it was quickly chased away by others — jet-black hair that curled at the nape of his neck, full mouth turned slightly down in worry, the handsome bronzed planes of his face; and his steel gray eyes, penetrating in their survey of her.

"Ma'am, are you all right?" He hobbled a few feet into the waiting room.

She knew she should respond, but in her

weakened emotional state she was at a loss for words. He towered over her. She slowly craned her neck upward past the leg cast, the narrow waist, the wide expanse of chest, the solid neck, to look into his puzzled expression.

Words suddenly flooded her mind. She bolted to her feet, nearly knocking the man backward. "I'm fine. Really, I am. Nothing to worry about, but thanks for asking. Sometimes I just need a good cry. It cleanses the soul, don't you think?" She paused, fluttered her hand in the air and continued, "Well, anyway, it helps me to keep going when things are a little tough." As suddenly as she started talking, she came to an abrupt halt at the shocked expression on the stranger's face. Her cheeks, beneath the white makeup, flamed as red as her clown nose, which she'd placed on the table next to her.

The best possible solution to this embarrassing situation would be a quick retreat, which would be near impossible in her oversize shoes. She sidestepped the giant, muttering, "Thanks again for your concern."

As she clumsily walked toward the exit, she was all too aware of his perceptive gaze on her back. She could imagine it singeing a path down her spine, and she shivered.

She was about to hasten into the hallway and disappear with a small thread of dignity still in place when he said, "You forgot something."

Her pride, she decided, and spun to face the man. In his grasp lay her red ball nose.

"Oh."

She started to snatch it from his outstretched hand when his long fingers closed around it. He shifted closer, positioning himself in front of her. Disconcerted, Tess found herself gulping.

"Here. The least I can do is fix your nose. I can't do anything, though, about the makeup."

He replaced the ball on her nose. The brush of his fingers against her skin was amazingly gentle and extremely warm, too warm. The touch stirred a fluttering in the pit of her stomach, a sensation she hadn't experienced for several years. The scent of sandalwood swirled about her, setting off alarm signals in her brain.

Tess stared into his gray eyes, caught by the intense look he directed at her. The ball was on her nose, but his fingers hadn't dropped away. Five seconds. Ten. An eternity. She was sure he could hear her heartbeat clamoring against her rib cage. It seemed to drown out all other noise.

When his gaze slid away from hers, his hand returned mercifully to his side. "No decent clown should be without a proper nose," he said, amusement causing his eyes to glint like diamonds in sunlight.

Suddenly, always quick to find humor in life, Tess laughed. "The penalty at the very least would be a pie in the face, which come to think of it might not be so bad since I skipped breakfast this morning. I guess I could compromise with a fruit pie and cover at least one of the food groups."

His grin reached deep in his eyes. "Haven't you heard that breakfast is the most important meal of the day?"

"Yes, and I don't usually miss any meals."

His gaze trekked down her length. "That's hard to believe."

She blushed again, something she was doing a lot around this stranger. "My name is Tess Morgan."

"Peter MacPherson." He held out his hand.

She slipped hers into his grasp, silently preparing herself for his long fingers to close about hers. Nothing, though, had prepared her for the electric feel his touch produced, as though she had stuck her finger into a socket. She quickly removed her hand from his grasp and edged back to give herself some breathing room.

"Are you visiting a family member?" Tess took another large step back, sandalwood-scented aftershave lotion still teasing her senses.

"No, just a friend."

"I hope it's not too serious."

"No, Tommy should be leaving in a few days."

"Tommy Burns? You visit him often?" She would have remembered seeing this man. He wasn't a person anyone could easily forget.

"Several times, but I usually come in the evening. Today I'm getting my cast off so I decided to see Tommy before I went to the doctor's office across the street. Do you know Tommy?"

"When I'm not wearing all this white makeup, I'm a nurse on this floor. I dress up several times a week to entertain the children. It's a kind of therapy I've developed." The waiting room was warm, and she knew it had nothing to do with the thermostat setting and everything to do with the man standing in front of her. She was sure her white makeup would soon start running in rivulets of sweat down her face.

"How long have you been doing that?"

"Six months, Mr. MacPherson."

13

He grimaced. "Please don't call me that. My friends call me Mac."

"Okay — Mac," she murmured, wondering what it would be like to be his friend. In the next second she realized being his friend would be too dangerous for her peace of mind. He was a bit too overwhelming for her.

"What made you come up with the idea of clown therapy?"

"I read about a program back East and thought it was a good idea."

"Why were you crying? Something go wrong today?"

His questions, so full of concern, pierced the invisible armor she wore to protect herself. She wasn't sure how to answer him. The truth was she hadn't cried in several years — wasn't sure why she had today. Maybe she was tired of fighting to keep everything in. But how could she tell a stranger that?

"Are you all right?" Mac moved closer.

Every fiber of her being went on alert at his nearness, though he was still an arm's length away. She nodded, trying to put together an answer that would satisfy him. "Not enough sleep lately. That's all," she finally said, realizing it was only a small part of the truth. She needed to focus on the good things about her job — the laughter, the smiles of joy and the reprieves she offered from pain. But she couldn't forget Johnny and the battle he might lose. The chemotherapy would work, and Johnny would go into remission.

"My, you are flirting with danger. No sleep and skipping breakfast," Mac said, a gleam dancing in his eyes.

"Tess." A man in a white coat stopped in the hallway and popped his head into the waiting room. "I just wanted to let you know Johnny is through with his therapy."

"How did it go?"

"Fine. He asked about you."

"I'll make sure to stop by and see him. Thanks for the update."

"A friend or patient?" Mac asked when the man left.

"Both." Tess thought about her struggle to get Johnny to smile this past week. She wasn't sure Johnny felt she was his friend, but whether he wanted her to or not she was going to stand by him.

"Johnny must be someone special."

"Why do you say that?"

"From the expression on your face when that man was talking about him."

"I've only known him a week, but he's become important to me in that short time.

I know I shouldn't become emotionally involved with a patient, but sometimes it's so hard not to. Johnny doesn't have any family. No one comes to visit him." And that was the reason she was drawn to him, Tess realized.

"How old is he?"

"Ten going on forty. He's a ward of the state." Tess glanced at her oversize watch that didn't keep time. "And if I don't get moving, I might be looking for another job. It was nice to meet you." She backed out of the room, glad she was hidden beneath tons of makeup and a red wig. If she stayed much longer, the man would have her whole life's history. It was too easy talking to him, and the last thing she wanted to do was become interested in any man, especially one who made her heart pound.

Tess started down the hospital corridor, her oversize shoes slapping against the linoleum floor. She was conscious of Peter MacPherson following her undignified exit with his sharp gaze. The hairs on her neck tingled, and the fluttering in her stomach intensified.

She had to get a grip on herself. Peter MacPherson was a man she would probably never see again. But she vividly remembered the warm, gentle touch of his fingers as he adjusted her round red nose. A gentle bear, she thought as she hurried to the nurse's locker room to remove her makeup.

After scrubbing the makeup off and dressing as a nurse, Tess left the locker room, determined to put the gentle giant out of her mind. She had no time in her life for a relationship. She was trying to piece her life together after the disaster in South America.

Pandemonium greeted Tess with a cold blast of panic when she approached the nurses' station.

"Tess, am I glad you're back. I was just going to page you," Delise said as she rushed up to Tess. "Johnny wasn't in his room when I went to check on him."

"Have you notified security? Looked all over this floor?"

"Yes. Yes. What should we do? We have medications that have to be given out."

"There's nothing we can do until we've given out the medications. I'm sure security will find him before we're through," Tess said in a calm, controlled voice, though her stomach muscles were tight as a fist.

What if Johnny had collapsed somewhere unconscious? What if he had a reaction to the therapy? What if — She had to block from her mind what could happen to

Johnny. He would be all right, she told herself as she put a bottle of medicine on the counter, closed her eyes and breathed deeply. But the antiseptic-laced air underscored in Tess's thoughts her fear that the child might not come out of this all right.

Mac stared at himself in the mirror in the men's room, an image of a clown stealing into his thoughts. A picture of her tear-streaked face with rivulets of black paint ruining her white makeup materialized in his mind. He remembered how she'd drawn in a deep breath, her hands clasped tightly in her lap to keep them from shaking. Slowly, while they had talked, she had pieced herself together, but the effort had left a vulnerability in her eyes that struck a chord deep in him.

What did she look like under all that white makeup and the red curly wig? He knew she was tiny, but that was about all. His curiosity was aroused. He wondered if he could fit his hands around her small waist. Shaking his head, he looked away. He would probably never know. Besides, he wasn't looking for a relationship of any kind.

He couldn't image finding anyone to take the place of Sheila. As he remembered his deceased wife, his throat constricted, making it difficult to swallow. In the past few years his life had changed drastically, and if he hadn't known the Lord's love, he wouldn't have been able to hold himself together for his daughter.

A noise behind him brought Mac up short. He'd thought he was alone. He glanced at the stalls, cocking his head to listen.

Crying?

The muffled sound filled the air. Someone whimpered. As quickly as his leg cast would allow, Mac hobbled to the stall at the far end of the bathroom.

"Are you all right in there?"

Silence. Even the whimpering stopped.

"Is everything okay?" Mac asked, alarm beginning to form in his gut.

A sound as if someone was falling launched Mac into action. He threw his body against the stall door, and it would have crashed open except that Mac stopped it. Carefully he swung the door wide. On the floor lay a boy, his pale face streaked with tears, his eyes fluttering closed.

After checking for a pulse, Mac stooped, picked up the child and cradled him. His small chest rose and fell with each shallow breath. Mac quickly carried the child from the bathroom down the multicolored corridor toward the nurses' station.

As Mac approached, he caught sight of a tiny nurse whom he somehow immediately knew was Tess. She was like a pixie with short brown hair feathered about her oval face, a cute turned up nose, a mouth meant for laughter and dark brown eyes he could imagine sparkling with mischief. It was those eyes that had given her away and drew him to her.

When she looked at him, her gaze widened, and her hand halted in midair. For a few seconds he saw fear in her eyes. Then a professional calm descended.

"Delise, notify Dr. Addison. Please come with me, Mr. MacPherson."

Mac started to correct her use of his name but stopped when he looked at her. He sensed she needed her professional facade, that it was the only thing that held her together. He followed her to a room across from the nurses' station, placed the boy on the bed, then backed away while Tess checked the child, her movements precise, efficient. But he saw the slight quiver in her fingers, as though the effort to be businesslike was taking its toll on her.

"I think he'll be all right," she said, the rigid set of her shoulders easing.

Mac started to ask about the child when the doctor came into the room. Mac quietly left to stand outside as if on guard at the door. He wanted to appease his curiosity about the child and the tiny woman who had touched him deep inside.

With his body propped up against the wall, he tried to ignore the ache in his leg. In his old profession he had certainly dealt with his share of pain. Massaging his tight muscled thigh, he focused his thoughts away from the dull throbbing and onto one nurse clown who captivated him more than he wished.

He remembered the helplessness he'd felt when he'd seen her in the waiting room crying, her face streaked with the evidence of her tears. A strong urge to comfort had drawn him into the room before he could stop himself. Her vulnerability had moved him, causing him to forget his losses for a short time. Seeing her again renewed his interest. He wanted to know what had put that look in her eyes that declared she'd seen more than her share of pain and suffering. He wanted to get to know her, ease the burden he sensed she carried.

Whoa, there, Mac. What do you think you're doing? Getting to know her? As a friend? Or, something more than that? He had more than he could handle right now in his life. Relationships were out. He'd been blessed by the Lord with one great marriage and wasn't looking for another.

The door swung open, and the doctor left the room. Mac waited another minute, then decided to go inside. He was never good at waiting, he thought with a smile.

Tess pivoted at the sound of the door swishing open. Her startled gaze took him in, running down his length, before she returned her attention to the boy on the bed. "Thank you."

Limping to the bed, he smiled at the child whose eyes were full of caution. "I'm Mac. I'm the one who found you. I just wanted to make sure you're okay."

For a full minute the boy stared at Mac as though he had sprouted wings and was going to fly about the room any second. "I'm okay." The child frowned and looked at his feet.

"Good. What's your name?"

Silence.

Mac glanced at Tess, a question in his eyes.

She started to say something when the child finally mumbled, "Johnny."

So this is the child Tess was concerned about, Mac thought, a tightness in his chest.

He was reminded of himself when he was Johnny's age, trying to carry off a tough, couldn't-care-less attitude. God had been his salvation. "Well, Johnny, I hope you'll let me come see you."

Plucking at the white bedsheet, the child shrugged. "Suit yourself."

"Johnny, I still have some medication to give out. I'll be back to see you in a bit. No more stunts, young man." Tess motioned for Mac to follow her from the room.

" 'Bye, Johnny." For some reason Mac was reluctant to leave. The child seemed so young, yet so old at the same time. Tess was right, in a way — Johnny *was* ten going on forty. But Mac suspected Johnny wanted to be ten years old and do whatever ten-year-olds did.

In the hallway Tess turned toward him. "Where did you find him? What happened? How did —"

Mac held up his hand. "Wait. Give me a chance to answer the first question."

Tess sighed. "Where was he?"

Mac couldn't take his gaze off the tiny frown that dulled her eyes and wrinkled her brow. He found himself wanting to smooth it away and make her laugh. Before he realized what he was doing, he raised his hand to her face and grazed his fingertips across her forehead as though that action would erase her concern.

Her eyes widened, and two patches of red fired her cheeks. "Mr. MacPherson, where?" she asked in a breathless rush.

"You look lovely when you blush."

Her brown eyes grew rounder, and she tried to step away, but the wall blocked her escape. Mac knew she was unnerved by the trapped look that appeared in her gaze. She doesn't hide her feelings, he thought and liked that. Sheila hadn't been able to, either. That comparison came out of nowhere and unnerved him.

"The men's rest room by the elevators," he finally answered.

"What happened?"

He supported himself against the wall with one hand braced by her head to take some of the weight off the leg with the cast. He could smell her scent, theater makeup and lilacs. "It's too long a story, and didn't you say you had medications to give out? I'll explain over dinner tonight." One part of him was as surprised at his invitation as she looked. It was as though there was another man inside him. Hadn't he decided he wasn't ready to get involved with another woman? Sheila had only been gone three years. And yet, he sensed a fragile composure in Tess that drew him to her. He found he was having a hard time resisting her.

"I don't date."

"That's okay. I don't, either. How about seven tonight?"

"I'm washing my hair. Sorry."

"Well, then, I suppose the story can wait until tomorrow night." The clean aroma of her hair perfumed the air.

"Nope. I have to scrub my bathrooms." A spark of mischief lit her brown eyes.

He laughed, leaning closer. "Then you tell me when."

Her head tilted to the side, she appeared deep in thought. A moment later she flashed him a sassy grin before ever so politely quipping, "How about we go out when pigs fly."

Chuckling, Mac watched her leave. He always liked a good challenge, and suddenly Miss Tess Morgan was daring him to discover the woman beneath the clown makeup and colorful uniform of a pediatric nurse. He limped toward the elevators. It was just as well she'd said no. He didn't have time for a relationship. He had a daughter who needed him and a large family that depended on him. No, sir, he had no time for a woman even if she was an intriguing, beautiful, caring one.

★ ★ ★

"Do you know who that is? Of course, you don't, or you'd have never let him leave." Delise pointed at the retreating figure of Peter MacPherson as he stepped onto the elevator. "He's *the* Mack Truck. He used to play for the Denver Broncos as a running back until he retired several years ago. He's a legend around here." Delise felt her friend's forehead. "Have you gone mad? Women would die to go out with him, but since his wife's death he's retreated from public life. From what I heard her death hit him quite hard. Left football. Started his own business, does something with a foundation and volunteers at a halfway house. Quite a family man, from everything I can gather about him. That's so appealing."

Tess shook her head, trying not to feel empathy for Peter MacPherson because that emotion would lead to others she definitely wasn't prepared to feel. "My, you could write his biography. Where in the world do you come up with all this?"

Delise fluttered her hand in the air. "Oh, you know, magazines, newspaper stories. The usual places. The bottom line is that he's one of the hottest items in Denver even if he doesn't want to be."

"You make him sound like a piece of merchandise."

"Oh, you know what I mean. Or has your eyesight gone with your brains?"

"They're both intact, thank you very much. Now, don't we have a job to do?" Tess walked to the counter and picked up her tray of medications.

"Did he ask you out?"

Tess realized she wouldn't get any peace or work done until she satisfied her friend's rabid curiosity. "Yes. And before you ask, I refused. Three times."

"I'm sure Dr. Smith can see you in emergency."

Tess sighed heavily. "Not every woman in this world is man crazy like you."

"Okay. I grant you maybe a visit to the shrink isn't necessary. Are you just playing hard to get? That might work, Tess. In fact, that's a brilliant idea. Be mysterious. Act uninterested. Keep him guessing." Delise snapped her fingers as she rattled off her advice.

"Whether I like it or not, I'm an open book. And I am not interested in that man." As Tess spoke, she tried to force conviction into her voice, but it lacked the ring of truth.

Tess didn't wait to hear her friend's response. She took her tray and entered the first room. If she was lucky, which she was beginning to doubt, Delise would tire of the subject of Peter MacPherson, and Tess could finish her shift without thinking again about that man.

But it wasn't Delise's questions that caused Tess to dwell on Peter MacPherson. She saw a boy with a cast on his leg, and she instantly thought about Mac and his gentle touch as he had replaced her clown nose. She saw an orderly who was over six feet tall, and she thought about Mac towering over her. And when she visited Johnny, he forced her again to think about the man.

"I would never have been found if it hadn't been for that man," Johnny declared as he twisted the white top sheet into a mangled ball of cotton.

"You're lucky he did."

"Why? I hate this place. I hate it!"

Tess swallowed the lump in her throat. "Hopefully you won't be here much longer."

"Then I'll just have to go live with some dumb old stranger."

"Mrs. Hocks is trying to locate your relatives." Tess hoped Johnny's case manager would find someone to take him in.

Johnny turned away from her onto his side and stared out the window, his shoulders hunched. "I don't have nobody."

Those words knifed through her, mirroring her feelings. She didn't have anybody, either, but that was the way she wanted it. Johnny needed a family. He needed love. Suddenly she was afraid he would pull another stunt like today. "You aren't going to try to run away again, are you?"

He didn't say anything.

"Johnny?" Tess moved to the other side of the bed and looked at the small child. His eyes were closed. She wasn't sure if he was asleep or faking it. It didn't make any difference, because if Johnny didn't want to talk, he didn't. Quietly she left his room, drained from the child's brief emotional outburst, from the day's events and especially from not trying to think about Peter MacPherson. He occupied her mind, threatening the fragile defenses she'd finally erected around her heart.

Chapter Two

A film of sweat covered Mac's body as he struggled to finish his leg exercises. Ten was all he could do with his mended leg. The soreness bore deep into him as he got up and limped to another machine. Absently he did arm curls as he mentally tried to psych himself up. It was only a matter of time before his left leg would be as good as new.

Three sharp raps at the door drew his attention. "Yes?"

His housekeeper stuck her head into the room. "Your sister is here."

"Which one?" Mac finished his last arm curl and put the weight on the rack.

"Casey."

"Does she have that troubled look on her face?"

" 'Fraid so."

"Tell her I'll be there after my shower. Fix her breakfast. She's way too thin."

"My thoughts exactly," Nina said as she closed the door to the exercise room.

Fifteen minutes later Mac hadn't stepped one foot into the kitchen when Casey started in. "You wouldn't believe the fight Mom and I had. All because I don't want to start college in the fall. You've got to talk to her, Mac. Tell her I'm an adult now and capable of making my own decisions."

"Do you think I might have some breakfast first? Say hello to my daughter." Mac scooped up Amy and whirled her around. The three-year-old giggled. When he started to put her in her booster chair, she said, "Do it again. Please, Daddy."

Not able to resist such a plea, he swung her around and around until he became dizzy. "Enough. I'm gonna be seasick, and we are landlocked, young lady." He settled his daughter in her chair and sat next to her, preparing himself for his sister's onslaught.

Casey gulped down half of her orange juice. "I don't want to go to college. Mom will listen to you."

While he watched Amy finish stuffing a piece of toast in her mouth, Mac took a bite of his omelette. "Why don't you want to go?"

"I want to go, but not this fall. I need some time to decide what I want to do with the rest of my life. I'm not like you, Mac. Everything in a neat little box."

He took his napkin and wiped his daughter's jelly-smeared face, then bent and kissed her nose. "Pumpkin, you're as good as new."

Amy jumped down from the chair and threw her arms around Mac's neck, kissing him on the cheek, then doing the same to Casey. " 'Bye, Aunt Casey."

Amy raced out of the kitchen. A minute later he heard the television. He glanced at his watch and realized her favorite show was on. He liked to watch it with her, but he needed to appease his sister or he would never be free.

"Casey, you think my life is in a neat little box?"

"Sure. You always know what you want and go after it. If it hadn't been for your determination, none of us MacPhersons would have had a chance at college. I just want my chance a year later than the others." Casey reached across the table and took Mac's hand. "Please talk to her. I don't want her mad at me, especially since Dad's death."

Mac felt the familiar emptiness at the mention of their father's death. He had not only been Mac's father, but his best friend, as well. Facing two deaths in the past three years had been very difficult, and without

God's love and guidance Mac wasn't sure he would have made it. He thanked the Lord every day for being in his life, his salvation when life overwhelmed him.

Casey squeezed his hand. "Please, Mac."

He focused on his sister, pushing the pain of his father's and wife's deaths to the background. "Casey, it's your decision. I'll have a talk with Mom."

She hugged him, a wide grin on her face. "Great! I knew I could count on you. The best time to talk to Mom is tonight at dinner. You're coming, aren't you?"

"Of course. I wouldn't miss Steve's birthday."

"You're the greatest! I'll let myself out. You just sit and finish your breakfast. 'Bye, Nina."

When Casey breezed out of the kitchen, Mac shook his head. He never had a moment's rest with his family. One child, three brothers and two sisters kept him hopping.

As his housekeeper poured his coffee, she said, "I know it's none of my business —"

"But you're going to make it your business anyway."

Nina ignored his interruption and continued. "Ever since you fell off that roof at the halfway house, you've been shut up here, working in that office of yours. You only go out to volunteer at the halfway house. You haven't gone out socially much in the past couple of months, not even to do things with your family. Now that the cast is off, get out. Enjoy life. Stop trying to do everything for everyone else. Do something for yourself. That's the way your father and Sheila would have wanted it."

"Whoa! Since when did you become Dear Abby?"

"Since I've been watching you draw in on yourself after Sheila's death. I think you used the accident to avoid seeing people socially, except family. I know how hard your father's death was on you, especially on top of the accident."

Mac scooted back his chair and stood. "I appreciate your concern, Nina, and I'll think about your advice. Now if you'll excuse me, I'm going to enjoy some time with my daughter, then I have a date at the hospital."

"A date at the hospital?"

"With a ten-year-old boy. So get that gleam out of your eye."

"Think about what I said," Nina called as he left the kitchen.

In other words, get a life, Mac thought as he sat next to Amy in the den. Until yesterday, when he had been drawn to Tess

34

crying in the waiting room, nothing much had touched him. It was as if the numbness was slowly fading, leaving in its wake a prickly awareness of one tiny woman.

There was absolutely no way Tess could sneak up on the children in the rec room with her oversize shoes announcing her approach from a mile away. But when she stepped into the room, ready to go into her clown routine, every child's head was bent over one piece of paper, and Peter MacPherson was in the middle of the group, drawing something on the sheet.

Is he a closet artist? Tess wondered, and moved into the room. Every child was looking at the paper and listening intently to what Mac was saying. Maybe Mac was a budding Rembrandt.

"Really!" one girl said in awe.

"Yeah. Here, let me show you what I mean. Brandon, you stand over there. . . ." Mac's words died in his throat as he straightened and looked into Tess's eyes.

Instantly a finely honed tension streaked through her as the heat of his gaze sealed the breath in her lungs. No matter how much she fought it, she couldn't deny the fact that this man heightened her awareness of how alone she was in this world, but that wasn't how she had planned it all those years ago when she had dreamed of her future. She had wanted a husband and a large family.

The girl who had been in awe came over to Tess. "Do you know who he is?"

"Yes, someone told me he used to play football for Denver," Tess said without thinking, her gaze still connected to his smoldering one. Oh, why in the world did she have to admit that she had been talking about him with someone?

"I strongly suspect, guys, this clown here doesn't appreciate the finer points of football." His statement was accompanied by a wickedly charming grin as he threw her to the wolves.

"You don't?" the oldest boy asked, his doubts about her sanity evident in his tone of voice.

Tess narrowed her gaze on Mac, wishing him bodily harm. "Tell you the truth, I've never been to a game."

"That's un-American!"

"You're joking!"

"Yeah, she has to be. Everyone has seen a football game."

Would a group of kids attack a clown for not having been to a game? Tess looked from one face to another and seriously thought about her chances of escaping in shoes four sizes too big. They'd tackle me at the door, she decided.

"I'm not into sports," Tess offered in the way of an explanation. It went over like water on a grease fire. "I've been out of the country for the past few years, and in high school I preferred to study on Friday nights," she added, aware that her explanations were bombing faster than bad jokes in a comedy act.

Her gaze fastened onto Mac's, and she wanted to lynch him. Crossing his arms over his massive chest, he was watching her and enjoying every minute of her discomfort with a huge grin on his face.

"I think she just needs someone to explain the finer points of the game to her," Mac finally said as all the children tried to tell her what she was missing at the same time. "I'll be glad to offer my services, say, over dinner tonight."

"Yeah, that's a great idea," several of the children said at once.

"Everyone should know about football," the oldest boy added.

Tess was speechless. Her refusal stuck in her throat.

"Come on. Say yes to him," the girl said.

Mac smiled an infuriating smile as he strode to her, leaned toward her and whispered, "Unless you're one of those people who judge something without knowing anything about it."

She stepped quickly away as if his breath had scorched her neck while struggling to control the shivering sensations spreading down her body. "I'm not!"

His smile broadened. "Then prove it. Have dinner with me. We'll be eating with a whole crowd of people, so you won't even be alone with me."

Tess swung her gaze from Mac to the children, all eagerly awaiting her answer. There really wouldn't be any harm in one dinner with him. He was the complete opposite of what she would be attracted to in a man, so she was perfectly safe. Wasn't she?

She looked him straight in the eye. "Fine."

He chuckled and whispered for her ears only, "It looks like a pig has just taken flight."

She smiled sweetly at him. "I'm sure anything is possible where you're involved."

"Is that sarcasm I hear in your voice?"

"Me? Never!"

His eyes twinkled. "It's interesting how you like to hide behind either a nurse's uniform or white makeup. Why is that?"

Tess felt the gazes of the children on them

and sidestepped toward the door. "Would you all excuse us for a moment?"

"You want to speak to me — alone?"

Tess took a deep, calming breath and said through clenched teeth, "Yes, please."

"Kids, we'll be back in a moment."

Out in the hall Tess leaned toward him and lowered her voice, conscious of the children in the room not three feet away. "Why are you here?" Don't you know I'm trying to avoid you? You aren't making that easy for me.

"I thought it was obvious. I'm visiting the children."

"Why?"

"I thought that was obvious, too. To spread a little joy and happiness, the same as you."

When he said "the same as you," Tess felt an instant bond with the man that she wanted to deny. She would have to endure their date that evening, but she didn't want to be around him anymore than was necessary. "Well, since you're spreading all that joy and happiness, I'll get back to my nursing duties." She started away.

"And miss all the fun?"

She glanced over her shoulder at him and saw six pairs of eyes glued to her. The children were framed in the doorway, intent on

Tess and Mac's conversation. She figured she had done enough entertaining today. "I'm sure there are some bedpans that need to be emptied."

The sound of her shoes slapping against the floor echoed down the hallway as she made her escape, embarrassingly aware of the gazes trained on her. She was seriously thinking of deep-sixing her clown shoes for some sneakers — a fast pair that could take her away from a very dangerously appealing man.

By the time Tess's shift was over, several hours later, she couldn't wait to get away from the hospital. She felt the walls closing in on her. She wished for the thousandth time she didn't throw herself so totally into whatever she was doing. It took a toll on her that once nearly did her in. She couldn't let that happen again.

Inside her apartment, Tess stripped quickly out of her sky blue pants and multicolored shirt, as though shedding her uniform would help her cope with the emotional treadmill she had been running on. But she felt wound up. She filled the bathtub with water so hot she had to force herself inch by inch into it. She eased back against the cold marble and laid her head on a plastic cushion, staring at the white ceiling, the evening with Mac looming ahead of her.

She wished again she'd somehow managed to refuse her date with Peter MacPherson. She wasn't looking for any kind of relationship. Once was enough for her. She'd left her broken heart in the Andes Mountains. Pain, buried and best forgotten, sliced into her, piercing her protective shell.

Determined to forget, she closed her eyes and blanked her mind. She concentrated on the heat seeping into her, stroking away her stress, the scent of lavender wafting to her, easing her tension. Slowly she drifted off. . . .

She faced a line of eleven huge men, bent on taking the football away from her. She crouched down, staring at the opposition with the meanest look she could muster. The ball was snapped. With her hands about the oblong pigskin, she dropped back, looked for a receiver and froze.

Mac hurled himself toward her. She ran forward, desperately trying to avoid him. Through the sea of men she rushed toward the end zone. She heard Mac behind her. With a quick glance back, she nearly tripped. He was only a yard behind her and gaining on her. She pushed herself to go faster, to cross the line before he plowed into her. Ten more yards. Five. She dove for the end zone at the same time she felt Mac's arms encase her. She fell forward, the air swooshing from her lungs as she hit the ground. Suddenly water was all around her, and she was gasping for breath.

Tess shot up in the tub, spurting, coughing. The man had entered her life, and she'd nearly drowned dreaming about him. She had to do something about this. She couldn't allow herself to care about another man, not after Kevin. They would have been married by this time with possibly a child on the way. Now all she had were memories. Always the memories.

Running her hands up and down her arms, Tess pushed away the images that threatened to invade her mind. Never again would she love like that. She would never allow herself to become involved with someone who could touch her heart. She couldn't live through the pain of losing again. It nearly killed her the first time. Being an all-or-nothing kind of gal was awfully hard on the emotions.

The water was chilly as she focused on the present. She shuddered from the cold, empty feeling that encased her like Mac's imagined embrace in her dream. She stood and toweled dry. She rubbed hard, as though she could erase the last vestige of her old self.

She was determined to build a life here in Denver completely different from her old one in South America.

She quickly dressed for her date, hoping that her casual attire of black slacks and a simple peach knit top would send the man the right message. Nothing serious.

By the time he picked her up, she'd paced a path in her living room that left a trail in the carpet. His warm greeting did nothing to ease her tension. While leaving her apartment, she found herself responding to his smile with one of her own and instantly wishing she could find fault. But he was the perfect gentleman, down to opening the car door for her.

As he started the engine, he peered at her and said, "You look beautiful. Quite different from the last time I saw you."

She remembered the incident in the playroom with the children and how he had maneuvered her into going out with him. She tried to muster some resentment toward the man but couldn't, especially when he looked at her as though she were the only woman in the world.

"How's Johnny doing?" Mac asked as he negotiated through traffic.

"Sulking most of the time. He has little to say when I visit him."

"I know. I stopped by his room before visiting the other children. I think he spoke three words to me the whole time I was there. I felt like I was carrying on a conversation with myself."

"Yeah, that's the way he is with everyone. I wish I could reach him. But things haven't been easy for him."

"Well, I haven't given up. I'll make a point to stop by again. I'm a pretty determined guy when something is important to me."

Tess could imagine his determination. He wouldn't have become such a good football player without it. But she was a determined lady, and he wasn't going to get her to do something she didn't want to do again. Even as she thought that, there was a part of her that realized she'd wanted to go out with him or she wouldn't have allowed the children to talk her into this date. That realization startled her.

When Mac pulled his car into the driveway of a house, Tess sent him a wary glance. "Do you want to show me your etchings?"

His laughter filled the small confines of the car, warming the already heated air.

44

Tess was caught by his silver molten gaze and held in its spell. This is a mistake, she thought frantically. It's way too dangerous for me to go out with him. He's too overwhelming.

"What if I said yes?"

"Then I'm not moving from this car." She felt herself being drawn into his web of male charm, held together by an incredible smile and the most beautiful eyes.

He grinned, his arm sliding along the back of the seat. "That'll be all right by me."

The air became unbearably hot. Tess felt prickles of heat slip down the length of her. She stared at that incredible smile of his that no human being had a right to and wanted to melt. She didn't know if she would be able to move from the car if her life depended on it.

Even though his arm didn't touch her, she was acutely conscious of it only inches from her. Her skin tingled as though electrical currents flowed between them. She found herself leaning closer to his arm along the back of the seat as if she needed to establish tactile contact with him. Oh, my, what's happening to me?

Suddenly she bolted upright, staring straight ahead, determined not to look at him. "I think you'd better take me home."

His laugh was low and full of warmth. "I never figured you for a gal who went back on a promise."

She threw him a surprised look. "I'm not. I went out with you. It was just an incredibly short date."

His chuckle danced along her nerve endings. "I suppose technically you've fulfilled your obligation to the children, but you're missing the intent of the date."

She quirked a brow. "Oh, and what is that?" she asked, confused by the way his laughter seeped into her bruised heart and demanded she forget everything but him.

His hand touched her shoulder, urging her back against the seat. "Stay and relax. All I want is for us to get to know each other."

The way he said "for us" made her breath catch and belied the meaning of his words. She wasn't good at this dating stuff, having done little of it in her life. She should never have let the kids at the hospital bully her into going out with Mac, even if there was a small part of her that had wanted to go.

"Friendship is about all I can handle in my life," he murmured, his voice low and throaty.

"Now I'm really comforted." Vividly aware of his hand near her shoulder, Tess

46

sat stiffly against the seat cushion. Her senses registered everything about him, his clean male scent, the silver gleam in his eyes, the dimples at the sides of his mouth when he smiled.

"If it would make you feel any better —" Mac stopped talking as a car pulled up behind them in the driveway and a man, woman and child got out of it.

The man approached Mac's car and bent down at the open window on the driver's side. "This has got to be a first. I don't believe it, Mac. You've never been early for anything. Turning over a new leaf?"

"Funny."

"Are you coming in or do you plan on celebrating out in the car?" The man's gaze slid to Tess then back to Mac. "I'll admit I wouldn't blame you."

"Tess, this obnoxious guy is my brother Justin. His wife, Mary, and their son, Justin Junior, are standing behind him."

"Brother?" Tess's voice was full of puzzlement. Her cheeks still flamed from Justin's comment.

"Yeah, I was about to tell you that this is my mother's house. We're celebrating my brother's birthday tonight, and the crowd I told you about at the hospital is my huge family."

"See you inside, brother dear. Don't take too long. Mom probably has her binoculars trained on you as we speak," Justin said.

Tess watched the couple and their son walk to the front door and go inside. She should be angry at the way Mac had deliberately misled her, but she couldn't muster the feeling. Relief washed over her. She knew in the brief ride to his mother's that she couldn't handle being alone with Peter MacPherson. She would have to remember that, and avoid the situation at all costs, she told herself as she clutched the door handle, needing to escape. She realized she didn't trust herself around Mac.

"Why the rush, Tess? The rest of the family isn't even here yet. Let's talk. Get to know each other. Believe me, once we hit that door, we'll get very little time to talk alone together."

"I know all I need to know." Is that my voice that sounds panic-filled? Tess, take deep breaths and calm down. So he makes your heart beat a bit faster and all your senses vibrate with awareness. It will pass, she assured herself, thinking back to the handful of guys she'd dated in her life and realizing she was definitely out of her league.

"There you go again, judging me before

you even know me."

She angled to face him in the small car. "I'm not judging you."

"Aren't you?"

"I'm just not interested in any kind of relationship."

"Even friendship?"

"Is that what this is all about?" Strangely, that was what frightened her. His offer of friendship was the most appealing aspect about him, she was discovering as she spent time with him.

"Yes and no. I'm not going to deny you interest me." His hand settled on her shoulder, kneading the taut muscles. "There's something between us even you can't deny. But, Tess, what I really want is to get to know you as a friend. No one can have too many friends."

Her eyes closed for a brief moment as she relished the feel of his hand on her, massaging the tension away, creating delicious sensations in her that went down to the tips of her toes. My gosh, she thought. He's good. Too good!

"I don't think casual is in your vocabulary." She pulled away, plastering her back against the car door, grasping anything — however fragile — to break the hold this man was weaving over her. "You say you want to be my friend, but something else is going on. Like you, friendship is all I can handle in my life right now."

"What happened, Tess? What are you running away from?"

Chapter Three

"I could ask you the same questions," Tess said, wanting to avoid the direction the conversation was headed in.

Sighing heavily, Mac opened the car door. "I think it's time we go in. Justin's probably right about my mother and the binoculars. I think I see sunlight glinting off glass from the living room window."

For some reason Tess couldn't let the question drop. "Are you avoiding my question? Why won't you answer it?" she asked as she faced him over the top of his car.

"Probably for the same reason you won't answer mine. It's not easy for the two of us to share our pain, is it?"

She blinked, nonplussed by the way he could hone in on what she was all about — and in such an incredibly short time. "I think you're right. We'd better go inside." She headed for the house.

A petite woman with gray hair opened the door before Mac could reach around Tess and put his hand on the knob. "I was beginning to think I'd have to send Steve out to get you."

"Mom, not everyone is here yet."

"But still, I wanted some time to get to know your friend before the rest of the horde descend."

With that declaration Tess found herself being studied by Mac's mother's sharp gaze, much like her son's.

"As you've probably surmised, this woman is my mother, Alice MacPherson. Mom, this is Tess Morgan."

Tess shook Alice's hand. "Pleased to meet you."

"The pleasure is all mine. When Peter called to tell me he was bringing a date, I was frankly very interested. Ever since Sheila —"

"Mom, where's Amy? I want Tess to meet my daughter."

"She's in the den with her cousins."

"I'll be back in a sec. I can trust you, Mom, not to say anything too outrageous while I'm gone."

"Why, son, never." Alice signaled for Tess to precede her into the living room. "I'll just get acquainted with your lady friend while you're gone. Take all the time in the world getting Amy. We'll be just fine,

Peter," Alice called as she winked at Tess. "I wager he'll be gone no more than a minute, if that long." Alice gestured toward the couch. "Are you from Denver?"

"No, I grew up in Maine but after my parents died, I decided on a change of scenery." Tess sat on the couch across from Mac's mother, feeling as though she were being interviewed by a pro and determined not to mention the year she'd spent in the Peace Corps in South America. That might lead to questions she didn't want to answer.

"I must warn you, in a moment this place will be chaotic. Do you have any brothers and sisters?"

Tess's chest felt tight. She drew in a fortifying breath and answered, "No." She had always wanted a lot of brothers and sisters. She was completely alone in the world. There had been a time when she had wanted a large family with Kevin. Now that wasn't possible, but the empty ache still hurt.

"Well, Tess, I'm not sure you missed out on anything," Mac said as he joined them in the living room, carrying an adorable-looking little girl in his arms. She had huge brown eyes and dark hair. "As the big brother, I have to put up with a lot of nonsense."

"Oh, sure, you think you're the only one who has suffered." Justin entered the room with another young man. "Steve, you tell our big brother how we have to constantly live up to his legend. It's very hard to at times."

"Justin, be kind to your older brother," Alice said with a laugh.

"Yeah, bro." Mac put Amy down and watched as his little girl walked to Tess.

Amy cocked her head, her brow knitted, and asked, "Who are you?"

"I'm Tess Morgan, a friend of your father's." The second she said the word *friend* she felt Mac's smug glance touch her face and wished she could stop her cheeks from flaming scarlet just with the thought of the man looking at her. She must learn to control her reaction to him.

"Daddy has a lot of friends," Amy announced, then wandered to her grandmother and sat next to her.

Tess was trying to decide what the little girl meant by friends when another man came into the room, quickly followed by a young woman. Suddenly the room was filled with people of various ages, from a baby to Mac's mother. Tess felt inundated. The people were all interested in her, kidding each other and enjoying the moment.

54

By the time everyone had introduced themselves, Tess counted fifteen people. She was never good at names, so she found herself reviewing their names as she listened to the conversation flowing around her.

Mac walked behind the couch and leaned over. "I have something I'd like to show you before dinner."

She smiled. "Those etchings finally?"

His chuckle was low, meant only for her. "Not here. Never any privacy. It's something outside. You just have to put your trust in me and come with me to find out."

The thought of putting her trust in Mac's hands didn't alarm her nearly as much as she thought it should. That knowledge sent a bolt of pure panic through her. Since South America she'd lost her ability to trust.

"Coming?" Mac asked, his hand extended toward her.

Fitting her hand within his grasp, Tess followed him from the living room, aware of a lull in the conversation. She suspected his family had stopped talking to watch them leave. Another blush tinted her cheeks as she realized they would be the topic of conversation after they left.

Mac confirmed her suspicion when he whispered into her ear, "I thought I would spice up their dull lives and let them talk about us for a while."

"Are you always so accommodating to your family?"

"Alas, you've found me out. I'm a doormat when it comes to them." He opened the back door and motioned for her to go first. "My daughter has already figured out how to wrap me around her little finger."

On the patio, the warm spring air felt good. Tess took a moment to relish the clean fresh air laced with the hint of honeysuckle. "What did you want me to see?" she asked when Mac came up behind her and stood close.

"This." He spread his arm wide to indicate the beautiful sky at dusk.

Mauves mingled with pinks and reds to feather outward to all reaches of the heavens. The light, cool breeze, carrying the scent of pine, ruffled the strands of her hair. The quiet just before night descended filled Tess with a momentary sense of tranquility she wished she could bottle.

The sunset was a vivid backdrop to the tall peaks. Tess loved the mountains. Standing on top of one was like standing on top of the world. That was one of the reasons she had chosen to live in Denver, even though the memories of the Andes

Mountains sometimes got to be too much for her.

"When I'm over at Mom's, I love to come out here in the evening and just enjoy the sight. This is what life's all about. God's creation," he whispered close to her.

Tess turned slightly so she could look at him, surprise in her expression.

He laughed. "Don't look so stunned. I can appreciate beauty as well as the next guy."

"Why did you play football?"

"I love the game. It gave me a lot."

"How did you break your leg — playing football?" She made the mistake of letting her gaze trail downward. As she took in his great physique, her face flushed. If she had to use one word to describe his body, it would be *powerful*.

"I've broken a couple of bones over the years, but I didn't break my leg this time playing football. I haven't played the game since I retired."

"What happened to your leg?" She turned and put some distance between them. Suddenly the cool air was warm, too warm. The space between them was filled with yearnings. She balled her hands at her sides, resisting the strong urge to run them over his massive shoulders. His body was a rock-hard force that spoke of his former profession.

"Nothing much. I was helping to roof a halfway house at which I volunteer and fell off the ladder. Now it's your turn. Why haven't you seen a game? You admitted to the children today that you know nothing about football."

"Kids take risks they shouldn't playing that game. I've seen firsthand some of the results as a nurse."

"Life's a risk."

"And life is much too violent without a game like football." She stared at the sunset quickly fading behind the mountains. She had seen enough violence in her life as an emergency room nurse, then as a Peace Corps volunteer in South America. An act of violence had claimed the man she'd been engaged to marry.

"Are you really being fair to the game?"

His presence behind her pulled her from memories that were always just below the surface. Potent power emanated from him, threatening to overcome any resistance she had. She steeled herself against that lure and said, "In high school I had a good friend who played football."

"And you never saw him play?"

"My studies were too important to me.

58

He asked me to, but sports wasn't my thing. His second year on the team, he caught the ball in the end zone for the winning touchdown. Three players tackled him. My friend never got up. He had to be carried off the field and to this day is paralyzed from the waist down."

"Football offered me a way to go to a good college. It opened up the whole world for me and consequently my family. It has given me a chance to use my status to spread the word of the Lord. Through my foundation I have been able to help a lot of people I wouldn't have been able to. Football gave me that chance." Mac came around to stand in front of her.

"What is your foundation?"

"I've used my connections in the sports world to raise money for the Christian Athletes Foundation, which I started a few years ago. Through this foundation I can fund certain projects. The Lord has provided for me. I want to provide for others."

"What kind of projects?"

"One of my more recent ones was establishing scholarships for students who don't have the money to go to college. I want to make sure others have the opportunity that I had through a good education."

"Education and football?"

"Yes, and football, but I don't want to talk about football. Let's talk about where we're heading, Tess."

The way he said her name, like a caress, was a silent plea for her understanding. She couldn't resist him. She wanted to understand him in that moment more than anything else.

"There's a connection between us I can't deny. I think you need a friend more than you care to admit." He reached up and cupped her face in his large hands, his touch electric. "Go out with me Saturday night. Just you and me. No family between us."

She laid her hands over his and stared into his silvery gaze, which radiated intensity. She felt lost as sensations she had never experienced washed over her.

"Will you go out with me?"

The question was a whisper between their mouths as he leaned closer to her, his breath anointing her lips. One of his hands fingered her hair then slid to clasp the nape of her neck. She was surrounded by him, his power shoving everything aside as her senses centered on him.

"Answer me, Tess," he whispered against her mouth.

An emotion deep inside her stirred, an emotion she'd buried forever, she thought.

"Yes, I'll go out with you."

She waited to see what would happen next, half anticipating him kissing her. His gaze locked with hers, and she felt a part of herself disappear.

"Mac, dinner's ready."

He lifted his head and muttered, "I'm gonna have to talk with my sister about her timing."

Slowly Tess's senses calmed enough for her to think rationally, to step away from him before she became lost again in his gaze. She welcomed the cooling breeze of evening as her heartbeat returned to a normal pace. He was a force she had never reckoned with or needed in her life. And in a moment of pure insanity she had promised to go out with him again Saturday night.

"I guess we'd better go inside or no doubt my whole family will come out to investigate . . . the sunset. They feel just because they're my family they have a right to know every little detail of my life, and then if that doesn't satisfy them, they make up a few tid-bits."

"And you probably love every minute of it."

He lightly touched the small of her back as she went through the door. It was a casual gesture, but nonetheless it unnerved her.

In the dining room the adults were seated at the long table. The children were at a smaller table in the living room. All eyes were on Mac and Tess as they entered the room and quietly sat, Mac at the head of the table and Tess to his right.

"Mac, will you do the honor of saying grace?"

Bowing his head, Mac clasped her hand as well as Casey's, who sat on the other side of him. "Heavenly Father, please bless this food we are about to partake and give us the wisdom to see our path in this life."

She felt comforted, and strangely a sense of peace descended, his fingers about hers and his simple prayer filling the room with his conviction.

"It's about time you two came in. I'm starved, and we've been waiting ages for you guys," Casey said as she started passing the platter of ham around.

Mac shot his younger sister a narrowed look. "Watch it, kid, or I'll forget our conversation this morning."

"Casey, you didn't go over to Mac's to get his help concerning college?" Alice asked, clearly upset by the frown on Casey's face.

"Yes, I did. He's the only one you'll listen to. Besides, it's his money that's sending me to college. I thought he should know I don't want it right now."

Tess ate her dinner while the rest of the family debated the merits of going to college right out of high school or waiting a year. She loved listening to the bantering among family members. She hated discovering Mac's generous nature when it came to his family. He had done so much for them, which, against her will, only endeared him even more in her eyes. It was going to be hard to stay away from the man, because she felt the same pull he did. And he was right. She did need a friend. She had avoided getting close to anyone for far too long.

After everyone had shared an opinion on the subject, Alice stood to cut the birthday cake. "Mac, what do you think?"

"It's Casey's life. It's her decision. It's something, Mom, she has to want to do." He took a sip of iced tea. "But I want Casey to know right up front that I believe a college education is the way for her to go when she's ready. It opens so many doors."

His mother gave the first slices to Steve and Tess. "Then it's settled. Casey, you'll have to find yourself a job if you aren't going to college right away."

Tess was amazed at how rapidly everything had been decided after such a diverse and lively debate. In the end it had been

Mac's opinion that counted. She got the impression he had become the father figure for all his brothers and sisters. What a wonderful burden to feel so needed by so many. Again she thought of her plans, which had died that day on the mountaintop in South America, and her throat constricted.

When the dinner was over, Kayla and Casey, Mac's sisters, started clearing the dishes while everyone else moved toward the living room.

"Can I help you?" Tess asked, needing to feel busy before her thoughts of the past took over.

"Sure. The more the merrier," Casey said and headed for the kitchen.

Tess picked up her plate and Mac's. He whispered as he left, "Don't believe a word they say about me. They've been dying to get you alone all evening. You just fell into their trap."

"Since I don't listen to gossip, you don't have a worry," Tess quipped as she strode away. The truth of the matter was she didn't want to know anything else about him. The more she discovered the more she liked, and she couldn't afford emotionally to become involved with anyone, especially him.

It didn't take one minute for the sisters to start the interrogation. "How did you two meet?" Kayla asked casually as she scraped food off the plates.

"Mac hasn't been too many places since the accident," Casey added.

"Sis, give her a chance to talk."

Tess smiled. Casey obviously didn't know all the finer points of an interrogation. "We met at the hospital."

"Hospital?" Kayla's forehead creased with a frown. "What was he — oh, I know. It must have been when he went to see Tommy." She looked expectantly at Tess for confirmation.

"Yes, he mentioned a little boy named Tommy."

"Mac hates hospitals, but he still visits the children whenever he can. Hospitals remind him too much of Dad and Sheila." Casey cut in with another tidbit of information.

It was clear to Tess that if she ever needed to know anything about Mac it was Casey she should pump for information.

"It was hardest on Mac having to watch Dad die slowly. They were so close," Casey continued as she opened the dishwasher. "Then of course, when Sheila delivered —"

"Casey, aren't there anymore dishes on the table?" Kayla asked, exasperated at her younger sister.

"No, I don't think so."

"Go check anyway. Then see if Mom needs anything. I think we can manage."

"But . . ."

Casey's protest died on her lips at the look her older sister gave her. She went meekly out of the kitchen.

"Casey is the kind of source the *National Observer* would love to get hold of." Kayla cast a glance at Tess. "But it is true Mac was pretty torn up about Dad."

In other words, Tess dear, you'd better have honorable intentions toward the man or get lost. "You have nothing to worry about from me," Tess answered the unspoken question as she began to load the dishwasher. My intentions are to get lost — just as soon as the next date is over.

Mac peered into the kitchen. "Tess, I'm sorry to interrupt you two getting to know each other, but I have an early day tomorrow. Ready to leave?"

"Yes," she answered, hoping she didn't appear too eager.

"Thanks for your help," Kayla said as Tess joined Mac.

"I figured when Casey came into the living room you were in big trouble," Mac whispered when they were alone in the hallway. "Kayla fancies herself my protector from the female population."

"So, you don't have an early day to-morrow?"

"I always have an early day. I think dawn is the best part of the day."

"Where's Amy?" Tess asked, hoping the little girl could act as a barrier between Tess and Mac on the ride to Tess's apartment. Tess was beginning to feel she needed all the help she could get to stay away from Mac. Her acceptance of a second date was proof she had a hard time resisting him.

"She's staying with her grandma tonight. So it's just you and me." He winked at her as he turned to say his goodbyes to his family in the living room and kiss Amy good-night.

Mac hardly gave Tess time to say her own goodbyes before he whisked her away from his large family. In the small car she was reminded of his powerful presence, which saturated every inch of the interior.

"I'd forgotten how overwhelming my family can be to a newcomer."

His family overwhelming? There's no way they compare to him. "Protective is a better word."

"We almost scared off Mary when Justin first brought her around to meet the family."

"I'm not easily scared," she said, then

wondered why she had.

He looked at her, his gray eyes penetratingly enticing. "I can see that."

The words, spoken in a husky timbre, tore at her already battered defenses. His study of her was so blatantly male that an ache deep inside threatened to rip the last of her defenses to shreds.

"You more than interest me, Tess. You're intriguing. One part of you is so innocent. The other I suspect has seen things that would make my stomach wrench. We'd better go. This certainly isn't the time or the place for this discussion."

Discussion? More like a temptation to forget everything she had promised herself, Tess thought and clasped her hands so tightly her knuckles turned white. But still she felt his lure — a lure that spoke of happier times, if only she could forget and forgive herself.

The drive to her apartment was done in silence. All of a sudden Tess felt physically and emotionally exhausted. She was beginning to wonder if she would have enough energy to walk to the front door.

At her apartment, Mac stood between her and the door. "I'll pick you up at seven. Dress casual."

"I can meet you at the restaurant."

"Is there a reason you don't want me to pick you up here?"

"Makes it seem like a date when aren't we just two friends going out to dinner?"

He stepped closer, slowly raising his hand toward her face. "Friends do go in the same car to places. And while we're on the subject of Saturday night, I'm paying for dinner. No Dutch treat, if that was what was going to pop into your head next."

"Fine," she murmured, deciding her brain had stopped functioning. She couldn't move an inch, so entranced was she by his presence. There was nothing friendly about what she was feeling.

When his fingers finally touched her cheek, she wanted to lean into him and seek his support because her legs felt so weak. For a few blissful seconds she wanted to forget her past, but reality was always just under the surface, ready to invade her thoughts. She felt again the pain of losing Kevin, of holding him in her arms as he lay dead. She felt again the anguish she had experienced when she had survived and no one else had.

Finally sanity returned, prodding Tess away from Mac. She fumbled for her key. "Thanks for a nice evening. It's late, and I do have an early morning." The words tumbled out in a coherent pattern that amazed her because inside she felt as though she were trapped in an English garden maze, lost and alone.

She finally found her key in the bottom of her oversize purse and quickly inserted it into the lock. "Good night. Thanks again."

Mac laid his hand over hers, the touch warm, intimate. "We're still on for Saturday?"

She needed to say no. She said yes, turned the knob and escaped inside. Leaning against the closed door, she listened as he left. With each step he took, she felt more alone, the way she wanted it ever since Kevin's untimely death. Then why did it bother her that such a nice man was walking away?

Chapter Four

Mac listened to the recording for a second time as though that would erase the words on the machine. "Mac, this is Tess. I'm sorry I've got to cancel our date this evening. Something has come up."

He frowned, rubbing the back of his neck while he played the message a third time. Yep, he was sure of it. Something was wrong. He could hear it in her voice. That settled it. He was going over there, and if she answered the door, he would act as though he hadn't received her message. The quaver underlining her words drew him to her. He had to go and make sure she was all right.

The pounding in Tess's head matched the pounding of her heart. She reread the letter from Kevin's mother, the fine, neatly written words leaping off the page as if the woman was in the room with her, shouting at her. Tess squeezed her eyes closed, remembering the last time she had seen Kevin's mother, at his funeral. She had created a hysterical scene in front of everyone in her congregation, wanting to know why Tess had survived when her son hadn't.

Tess's hand shook as she carefully placed the letter on the coffee table then switched off the lamp next to the couch. Relieved that the shadows of dusk crept into the room, she stretched out on the sofa, hugging one of the throw pillows to her chest. The letter had restated the woman's ramblings at her son's funeral. Again.

Tess stared at the ceiling until the blackness totally swallowed the light and she couldn't see anything. She kept her mind blank, needing to think of nothing at the moment. But slowly thoughts slipped inside to torment her. The rebels had left her to die, but she hadn't. She had survived when no one else had.

For the past two years she had run from what had happened at the mission, but it was becoming more difficult to hide from the memories, to forget — to forgive. Weariness weaved its way through her, making her eyelids droop. Her grip on the pillow eased as the lure of sleep engulfed her.

Tess threw her head back and took a deep breath of the crisp mountain air, clean, fresh.

Not a cloud in the sky, and the temperature a perfect sixty-five. What a glorious day! She looked at the ring on her left hand, its diamond glittering in the sunlight. In a few short months she would be married.

Someone called her name. She glanced up.

Kevin stood in the middle of the Indian village nestled at the bottom of a mountain. He waved to her, a wide grin gracing his mouth. She started toward him, eager to share her news about the little girl brought in that morning who was finally responding to treatment.

Crack!

Kevin's smile crumpled as he collapsed to the ground, a bright red spreading on his white shirt.

She froze, her eyes widening at the pool of blood around Kevin. Then her world completely shattered as a horde of rebels from a mountain stronghold descended on the village like a swarm of locusts.

Screams pierced the clear mountain air. The scent of gunfire accosted her and propelled her forward — toward Kevin. Ten feet away. Five.

The insistent ringing wormed its way into her nightmare, pushing Tess toward wakefulness. She blinked, trying to focus on the present.

The sound persisted, filling her mind with urgency. She rolled to her feet and fumbled for the switch on the lamp next to the couch. Brightness flooded the room, causing her to blink again.

Shaking the haze of sleep from her mind, she started for the door. When she peered out the peephole, she saw Mac standing on her front porch and immediately opened the door, forgetting to mask her dismay at seeing him.

"Are you ready —" His smile of greeting died when he looked into Tess's pale features, her eyes lackluster and pain-filled.

"What's wrong, Tess?"

She combed her fingers through her hair, staring at a place over his shoulder before swinging her gaze to his. "I left you a message. I can't —" Her voice broke, and tears welled into her eyes.

Mac stepped into the apartment and shut the door behind him. He drew her into his arms and pressed her head to his shoulder. "I know. I ignored the message." He'd had every intention of letting her believe he hadn't received the message, but suddenly it was very important for him to tell the truth. "I could tell something was wrong. That's when a person needs a friend the most."

The way he said *friend* made the tears flow. She had been running for the past two years and had avoided getting close to anyone. Now suddenly this man wasn't allowing her to remain aloof, and she was found she didn't want to. She needed to know someone cared, if only for a short time.

She felt the dampness of his shirt against her cheek and the strong stroke of his hand down the length of her back. She smelled his scent, sandalwood and soap. She heard the steady beat of his heart beneath her ear and felt as though its soothing rhythm could erase the remembered sounds of gunfire that echoed through her mind. And for a while it did. It had only been one of her nightmares. This was reality. Denver. The children she helped. Peter MacPherson.

"Do you want to talk about it?"

Tess shook her head, her throat still too tight to say anything, her fragile emotions raw and near the surface.

He continued holding her for a few minutes while she drew in calming breaths and tried to right the chaos she had felt deep inside since that day her life had changed. When she pulled back, still loosely fitted in his embrace, she peered at him through red-rimmed eyes.

"I must look a sight." She swiped her hand across her cheeks to rub away any evidence of her losing control. This was the second time he had found her crying in their short acquaintance.

His mouth quirked in a smile. "Maybe a sight for sore eyes." His arms fell to his sides.

Again she fingered her hair, trying to bring some order to its unruliness, and returned his smile. "If this is your way of cheering a gal up, it's working."

"Good, that's what I came over here to do. Give me some coffee and I'll regale you with stories of my family. That ought to make anyone thankful they don't have to walk in my shoes."

"I hear your teasing tone, and don't forget I've met that family. They are dears."

He tossed back his head and laughed. "Dears? My, I've never heard them referred to as dears."

His infectious laughter spread through her, warming her inside. She imagined his younger brothers, all over six feet and broad-shouldered like him, and knew they wouldn't want anyone to think of them as dears. "Well, at least your mother, daughter and sisters are."

"Oh, but the trials and tribulations of being the head of a large family. Casey was over at the house first thing this morning wanting me to help her find the perfect job. I said something about working at the foundation for me, and she immediately said no. She wants a job, but she's being awfully picky about it. Says she can't work for me."

"What does she like to do?"

"She likes working with people and she's good with computers."

"We have an opening on our floor for a unit secretary if she wants to apply at the hospital."

"I'll mention it to her. She loves children so she might go for it."

"Come on into the kitchen. I'll put some coffee on and even fix us something to eat." She stopped after only taking a few steps and turned to him. "That is if you haven't had anything for dinner yet."

"Nope." Mac followed her. "Do you have a roommate?"

"Yes, but Delise is gone for the weekend. She went to see her parents in Aspen. She wanted me to go but I —"

"— had a date."

She paused at the counter and glanced over her shoulder at him. "Well, yes, that, too. But I promised Jan I would work for her tomorrow. She needed some time off while her son was home from college."

"How long have you been a nurse?"

"Seven years."

"Have you only been a pediatric nurse?"

"No." Tess turned her attention to making the coffee, concentrating on keeping her hands from trembling.

"What else have you done?"

She hadn't heard him approach, but he stood right behind her. She sucked in a deep breath and held it for a long moment. "A little bit of everything," she finally answered, aware that her voice quavered.

He laid his hand on her shoulder and squeezed. "I'm sorry. Have I hit a taboo subject?"

She swallowed hard. "My first job as a nurse was in the emergency room in a large city hospital. I saw more that year than a lot of people do in ten years. I moved around after that, but I've decided working with children is what I want to do from now on."

He positioned himself next to her, lounging against the counter with his arms crossed over his chest. "I see your fascination with clowns extends to your home."

After putting the coffee on, Tess leaned next to him and looked about her. Her clown collection overflowed from the living room into the kitchen as well as her bedroom. "I started collecting them when I was

78

a little girl. I can't go by one in a store and not buy it."

"I can tell. How many do you have?"

"I stopped counting after a hundred."

"Well, I know what to get you for your birthday."

"Yeah, I'm easy to buy for." She tried to ignore the implication of his teasing statement, but she couldn't. It suggested they would have a future. She saw how at home he appeared in her kitchen, and her wariness pushed to the foreground.

"Of course, a friend has to keep straight which clowns you have, and I'm sure there will come a time when you'll have everything there is to have."

She shoved away from the counter. "I always say if you're going to do something you might as well do it right."

"An all-or-nothing kind of person."

"Yeah, I'm afraid so. I tend to jump in with both feet."

"What happens when you discover there's no water?"

Tess went to the refrigerator, some of life's painful lessons washing over her. "It hurts when I land."

One side of his mouth lifted in a self-mocking grin. He bent and rubbed the leg that had been in a cast the week before.

"Boy, I can attest to that."

She chuckled, glad he was putting the conversation on a light note. Searching her refrigerator, she came up with the makings for ham and cheese sandwiches.

"Can I help?"

"You can set the table while I make the sandwiches. The plates and glasses are over there, and the silverware is in that drawer." Tess pointed with the tip of a butter knife.

While she prepared their light dinner, she listened to Mac move about her kitchen as though he had visited her often and knew where everything was. Again the impression he was comfortable, at home in her apartment besieged her. That thought brought a halt to her movements as she slid a glance at the man who dominated any room he entered. He filled the space with his muscled body, but mostly his presence radiated confidence and determination. He had a direction to his life that Tess envied. Once she'd had a path to follow, but she'd lost her way.

"The coffee's done. Do you want any?"

His question broke into her thoughts. "Yes, please." She hurried to finish the sandwiches, realizing she was thinking too much.

When she sat at the table, the scent of brewed coffee wafted to her. She inhaled the fragrance, much too aware of the man next to her. After adding sugar to the coffee in her mug, she lifted it to her lips and took a sip.

He picked up the salt and pepper shakers and examined them. "Clowns. My daughter would like these."

"Most kids respond to clowns."

"Is that why you started your clown therapy?"

"Yes. I wanted a way to take their minds off why they were in the hospital. Most of the time I succeed." Tess began to eat her sandwich, enjoying the sharp taste of aged Cheddar cheese and the tang of the mustard.

"But not all the time?"

"Every once and a while I run across a tough cookie."

"Like Johnny?"

"Yeah, he's been a challenge."

"He's had a lot of hard knocks for a ten-year-old." Mac popped a potato chip into his mouth, then took a bite of the ham and cheese.

"I just hope Mrs. Hocks finds a relative for him to live with."

"Who's Mrs. Hocks?" Mac washed his meal down with a swallow of coffee.

"His case manager."

81

"What's gonna happen to him in the meantime?"

"He'll live with a foster family. He leaves the hospital on Monday afternoon."

"What does Johnny think about that?"

"He tells me he would rather be on the street taking care of himself."

"Do you believe him?"

Tess tilted her head to the side and thought about the last time she saw Johnny, his mouth set in a defiant frown. "Yes, I'm afraid he believes he's better off by himself. He's been shuffled between foster parents before."

"Then, do you think he'll run away?"

"He has a habit of doing that when faced with something he doesn't like."

Mac speared her with a sharp gaze. "Most people do."

She was close to squirming under his unrelenting stare. She felt as if he had delved into her mind and glimpsed her innermost thoughts. She dropped her glance to her plate and fingered what was left of her sandwich. "Sometimes running away is the best thing for a person. The only thing."

"Do you really believe that? Do you think that's what's best for Johnny?"

She lifted her gaze to his probing one. "No, it isn't. He needs a home, someone to love him. But he doesn't need to be shuffled between different foster parents just because he may be a little difficult."

"I agree." Picking up his half-eaten sandwich, Mac took another big bite and chewed slowly, the whole time his attention fixed on her face, a thoughtful expression in his eyes.

She blushed, wishing she could read what was in his mind. Or maybe she didn't want to. The flare of interest was more than she could handle. She wanted no complications in her life, and Peter MacPherson was definitely a complication. She looked away before he saw more than she wanted him to see.

Mac covered her hand next to her plate, forcing her attention to him. "I hope his case manager will find a relative to take him in."

"They've been looking for over a year, since he became a ward of the state. There may not be anyone. Johnny doesn't say much about his family. He won't talk about his mother, who died last year, and I don't think his father was ever around much. From what Mrs. Hocks has said, he abandoned them long ago." She slipped her hand from Mac's grasp, feeling the imprint of his fingers as though it was a brand.

"No one should have children unless they are willing to take care of them. They're too precious to ever take lightly."

She didn't want to get into the subject of having children. That possibility had vanished for her when Kevin had been taken from her. Their dream of a large family was just that, a dream. Twisting her napkin in her lap, she searched for a topic of conversation that wasn't so painful. "Tell me about your work at the halfway house. You said you were fixing the roof and fell off the ladder when you broke your leg. Do you work there often?"

"I don't usually do those kinds of things at the halfway house, and after that accident, I'll make sure I hire someone to do it from now on. Being a handyman isn't my area of expertise."

"What is?"

"I usually hold counseling sessions several times a week. I spend most Monday, Wednesday and Friday afternoons there."

"Counseling? You're a counselor?"

"I majored in psychology in college, and after I quit football, I went back for my masters."

"I thought you were a businessman."

"That, too. I have investments and the

84

foundation to look after. But my love is counseling. I wish I could do more, but I do have those other obligations that are important to me, too."

"Why the halfway house?"

"I've seen what drugs can do to people."

"So have I. Some of those emergencies I told you about my first year were drug related. Not a pretty sight."

"Then you understand why I have to do something. I had a friend in college who got involved with drugs. I couldn't help him. He died of an overdose. I promised myself then I would make a difference."

"I think that's why I became a nurse. Like Casey, I like people and found I wanted to help." Tess relaxed in her chair and sipped her coffee. She liked Mac a lot. He cared about others and wasn't afraid to show it. "In school I was good at science and for a while thought about being a chemist. Then I decided in college that I didn't want to be stuck in a lab, working with test tubes all day. I wanted to work with people, particularly children."

"I think my most rewarding work is with the youth group at church. Some of the most confusing, trying times for children are when they are in middle school. I find myself looking forward to teaching them each week about the power of the Lord's love. It has sustained me through a lot of rough times."

The devotion and intensity emanating from Mac reminded Tess of Kevin. She frowned and looked away, not wanting to remember anymore that evening. "I'm glad God is a comfort to you." She finished the potato chips on her plate as though it was important that she eat everyone of them.

"What happened, Tess?"

"Let's just say I was abandoned in my time of need and leave it at that." She stared at her empty plate.

"If you want to talk, I'm a good listener."

"The counselor in you?"

"The friend in me."

"There's nothing to say. I would rather leave my past in the past."

"Well, did I ever tell you about the time the kids in the youth group had me skateboarding in the parking lot?"

She shook her head.

"I crashed and burned several times. I'm surprised I didn't break my leg that day. I will say those kids make me feel young."

Tess laughed. "You are young."

"Sometimes when my body protests and creaks, I don't feel young."

"How old are you? Thirty-two? Thirty-three?"

"Thirty-four."

"Oh, what an old man you are," she teased, enjoying the heightened color that crept into his cheeks.

"Okay. Turnabout is fair play. How old are you?"

"Didn't your mother tell you never to ask a lady her age?"

"Yes. How old are you, Tess?"

The mischievous gleam in his eyes made her heart beat faster. "Twenty-eight. *Much* younger than you."

"I'm robbing the cradle."

She tensed, realizing how easy it would be to fall in love with Mac. She wouldn't do that to herself again. "But we aren't dating."

"This was supposed to be a date. Remember?"

"Yes, but I canceled."

"I'm here. I didn't let you cancel."

"Well —" She couldn't think of anything to say to that declaration. She snapped her mouth closed and stared at him.

"But you're right — this really isn't a proper date. So you owe me one. Let's say next Saturday night, and don't leave any messages on my answering machine begging off."

Tess rose, busying herself by taking her plate and cup to the sink. "I'm sorry. I am busy next Saturday night."

"Washing your hair?"

"No."

"Cleaning your bathroom?"

"No, I'm working. I'm pulling double shifts for the next few weeks. We're short-handed at the hospital."

She listened to the scrape of his chair across the linoleum, then his footsteps covering the distance between them. He placed his dishes in the sink next to hers, his arm brushing against hers. Tension whipped down her body as she turned on the water, her hands trembling.

"Thanks for the sandwich. I'd better go. I'll be seeing you."

Surprised — and somewhat disappointed — that he gave up so fast, Tess dried her hands and followed him from the kitchen. "I appreciate your understanding about this evening." She opened the front door and leaned on it while he stepped over the threshold.

Turning, he smiled. "Anytime. Good night, Tess."

She watched him walk toward his car, perplexed at her reaction to him leaving so abruptly. Wasn't that what she wanted? To be left alone? Then why did it bother her that he didn't fight longer for a date with her?

Mac sat in his car staring at the closed door to Tess's apartment. Like her heart. Closed to the Lord. Closed to people who cared about her.

Heavenly Father, give me the guidance and strength to help Tess through her hurt and pain. She needs You. Help me make her see that.

As he started his sedan, he suddenly knew what he would do to help Tess. In the dark, he smiled.

Chapter Five

Tess stared out the picture window that overlooked the hospital parking lot, the mountains in the background. "Where is Johnny?"

"They'll find him, Tess." Delise laid a reassuring hand on her shoulder. "Where would a ten-year-old boy go?"

"I knew he was going to run away."

"And you told Mrs. Hocks your fears. That was all you could do."

"He's been gone for two days. It still gets cold at night here."

Delise's tightening clasp on Tess's shoulder conveyed her support. "I know. About all we can do right now is pray."

Tess rejected that option. She had tried it once, and it hadn't helped. She whirled. "I can do more than pray. I know that when my shift is over I'm hitting the streets again."

"You were out searching for Johnny the past two evenings. You don't even know where to look. Let the police handle this."

"I can't sit home and wait. I have to do something. Even if it's driving around looking, it's better than sitting home and waiting for the phone to ring." Or worse, the phone not ringing. Tess ignored her friend's worried look as she headed to the nurses' station.

Delise followed her. "I can't go with you tonight. I'm working a double shift. I don't like you going out looking by yourself. Some of the places we went last night weren't too safe."

"Delise, I'm —" Tess pivoted to face her friend and halted in midsentence. Mac stood behind her roommate. "I'm a big girl. I can take care of myself." Some of her words lost their punch as she stared at Mac.

Delise glanced over her shoulder at him. "I'm glad you're here. Talk some sense into her. She won't listen to me. She shouldn't go out by herself looking for Johnny."

"What happened to Johnny? Did he run away?"

Tess nodded.

"How long ago?"

"Two days." Seeing Mac made Tess's heart lift. Somehow she knew things would be okay.

"I'll go with you. When are you off?"

"In an hour. Why are you here?"

91

"I brought Casey in for an interview about that unit secretary's job. You should have called me and told me about Johnny disappearing two days ago."

"I —" Tess didn't have anything to say to that gentle scolding. She'd dialed his number once and hung up. She'd known he would help and that he would want to know about the child's disappearance, but she didn't think she could handle being around Mac. He overwhelmed her, and this situation with Johnny made her emotionally vulnerable.

"Tell you what. I'll call Mrs. Hocks, talk to her and see what I can find out. Then I'll be back to pick you up in an hour. We'll go from there."

"I'll be ready," Tess murmured as she watched him stroll away.

Delise whistled softly. "My, what a take-charge kind of guy. He's a keeper."

And that was what Tess was afraid of. How do you resist an irresistible guy?

"I'll take some more of that coffee." Tess held her empty mug out for Mac to refill. "I know it's April, but it's cold out there." A shiver flashed up her spine as she cradled the warm cup between her hands and stared out the windshield. She savored the aroma

92

of the hot brew and relished the steam wafting over her face in waves.

Then she thought of Johnny, out in the cold by himself, and frowned. "Why did he do it? Leave a safe haven for this?" She gestured toward the vacant parking lot.

"He thinks he's alone. We'll have to show him he's not."

"They're talking about a chance for snow tonight." Another shiver assailed her.

Wind blew the limbs of the trees, shaking the tender new leaves in its angry grasp. Pieces of trash swirled across the deserted parking lot, the glare of the street lamp nearby casting a harsh light about Mac's car as though it were a spotlight.

"Where else do you think we should look?" Tess took a tentative sip of the hot coffee.

"I'm fresh out of ideas. We've been to every place Mrs. Hocks could think of. Of course, the police have already checked those places, too, but it didn't hurt to look again."

"And again, if need be."

"Tess, you need to prepare yourself in case they don't find Johnny." Mac caught her gaze and looked long and hard into her eyes. "He's street smart. There are a lot of places a kid can hide in this town."

"He's sick and weak. We've got to find him."

Finishing his coffee, he started the engine. "Then we'd better get moving. We'll drive around the area where the police found him the last time he ran away. Maybe we'll get lucky, Lord willing."

Tess listened to the strong faith in Mac's voice and wished she had it. But it hadn't been the Lord who had rescued her in South America. It had been her hard determination to stay alive in the face of tough odds. That same determination came to the surface as Mac steered his car onto the streets.

"Johnny's lucky to have someone like you on his side," Mac said, making a turn onto the road where the police had found Johnny a few weeks before.

"I wish I could take him into my home, but as you know, the apartment I share with Delise is small. And besides, we both work quite a bit. Johnny needs someone there for him, especially at the beginning."

"Maybe Mrs. Hocks will find a relative."

"I'm not sure that's the answer. Johnny has told me he doesn't want to live with relatives he doesn't know. To him they'd be no different than foster parents."

The blare of Tess's cell phone cut into the silence. Startled, she jumped. "I forgot I left it on." She fumbled in her purse and pulled it out, flipping it open. "Tess here."

"Johnny's been brought into the hospital. He's down in the emergency room right now. I thought you'd want to know."

"We'll be right there, Delise. Thanks for calling." Tess clicked off and told Mac about Johnny.

He made a U-turn in the middle of the road and headed for the hospital. "At least he'll be warm tonight."

"And from now on, if I have anything to do with it," Tess said, not sure how she was going to follow through with her vow.

"He's lucky he didn't freeze to death." Tess stared at Johnny asleep in the hospital bed, his face pale and thin, dark circles under his eyes. "How do I make him realize he's not alone, Mac, that there are people who care about him?"

"With the Lord's help." Mac came up behind her.

She felt his presence down the length of her even though he didn't touch her. She stiffened, resisting him, resisting his words. "I'm going to depend on my powers of persuasion. You can depend on God."

"I've asked you before what happened to make you turn away from the Lord."

"He let me down when I needed Him the most."

"Are you so sure of that?"

Tess spun and took a step back to put some space between them. "Most definitely." She kept her voice low, aware of the child in the bed behind her.

"Do you say that because He didn't do what you wanted? Sometimes, Tess, we have to put our faith in the knowledge that our Lord knows what is best, not us."

Her fingernails dug into her palms. "All I wanted was for a good man who served God to live to continue his ministry."

Suddenly the room seemed to stifle her. She fled into the hallway and leaned against the wall, drawing in shallow breaths. The click of the door closing brought her head up. She stabbed Mac with a narrowed look and hoped he got the hint. She didn't want to talk about it anymore. The pain speared her heart, and she bled all over again as though the wound was fresh.

"Tess —"

She held up her hand. "Please, Mac. I didn't say that so we could start a discussion."

"I stand by what I said. We don't always know what the Lord wants of us or our loved ones." He lifted his hand toward her.

"Now, let me walk you to your car. You need to get some sleep."

Combing her fingers through her hair, she avoided his touch, knowing its enticing lure. Instead, she attempted a smile that she knew failed and asked, "Gee, do I look that bad?"

"No, but you do look exhausted. Those double shifts are beginning to add up."

"I'm staying. I need to reassure myself that Johnny will be here tomorrow morning. That he won't somehow get up in the middle of the night and escape before I can talk to him."

"You can't be with him all the time. There comes a time when you have to put faith —"

She pressed her fingers against his mouth and instantly regretted touching him. She dropped her hand and moved away, her back coming in contact with the door into Johnny's room. "Don't say it. I'm staying. Good night, Mac."

"Then I'll stay with you and keep you company."

"You have a family at home."

"I have a live-in housekeeper who takes excellent care of Amy. She'll be fine. You, on the other hand, I'm not so sure about."

"You aren't my keeper."

"I know that. You've made it perfectly clear to me and everyone else that you want to stand on your own two feet."

Her chin came up a notch. "And what's so bad about that?"

"I hate to say a cliché, but I'm going to anyway. No man, or in this case woman, is an island. You aren't alone, just like Johnny isn't alone. How can you make Johnny see that if you don't believe it?"

His words struck her with the truth. She didn't have an answer for him. Most of her life she had depended on people around her to complete who she was, first her parents, who died one after the other, then Kevin, who was murdered. She gave Mac a look that told him to back off. "I depend on no one for my happiness. Johnny will need to learn to depend on himself, too, when the time is right. The time isn't right for him."

Determined not to let her emotions get the best of her, Tess decided the only thing she could do was ignore Mac as much as possible. Behind her she fumbled for the handle and quickly opened the door to slip inside Johnny's room — she hoped alone. The sound of Mac entering behind her made her stiffen her resolve to put as much distance between them as possible. But then she realized the only comfortable place to sit down was the love seat on which Mac was already seated. Her legs trembled from exhaustion. Reluctantly she eased down next to him after pacing the small room for fifteen minutes.

In the dim light the hard lines of Mac's face were softened, and she could see the weariness etched into his features. She fought the urge to brush her fingers over those features as though that action could erase the deep lines of fatigue. Clenching her hands in her lap, she sat up straight, her shoulders thrust back.

He touched her arm. "If you don't relax, I'm afraid you're going to shatter. If you sit back, I promise not to think you're depending on me."

She whipped her head around, meaning to say something scathing, but the words lumped together in her throat. His look melted her resolve, and she realized he was only trying to help her and Johnny.

He smiled, his eyes sad. "It's gonna be a long night, Tess."

The tender concern in his look moved her more than she cared to acknowledge. It had been a long time since she'd felt such companionship. His offer of friendship was a temptation she found unable to resist. She leaned against the cushion, her body nestled in the crook of his arm. "I'm afraid you're right."

"Then you and I should be as comfortable as possible on this hard, incredibly small couch."

She grinned at him. "I think you have a point, but this love seat is much better than that chair over there."

Mac inspected the chair with a wooden back and a cushion that had little padding. "True." His attention returned to Tess. "What would you like to talk about?"

His whispered question flowed over her in enticing waves, beckoning her to get to know him better. Danger lay in that direction. "The weather? It's beastly out there for this time of year."

"Oh, yes, beastly. But you're from Maine. You should be used to the cold."

"I'm finished with winter and definitely ready for summer."

"Well, now that we've explored the weather, what else do you think is a safe subject?"

"Not politics."

"Nor religion."

Tess started to sit up when Mac's hand on her shoulder stopped her.

"I shouldn't have said that, Tess. But one day I hope you will open up to me and tell me what has put that look of sadness in your eyes. Did I tell you Casey got the job?"

She latched onto the change in subject matter, easing again into the crook of his arm. "I'm glad she will be joining us. We have a great group of people working on this floor."

"She's excited and relieved. Mom hasn't let up since the birthday party about her getting a job. She doesn't believe in idleness."

"What's Casey been doing since high school graduation?"

"A little bit of everything. She doesn't know what she wants. Ever since she graduated from high school in December, she has been going from one job to another."

"She's still young. A lot of young people her age don't know what they want to do."

"Were you like that?"

"No, I always wanted to be a nurse. How about you? Did you always want to play football?"

"I love the game. I got paid well for doing something I enjoyed. Can't beat that."

"Then why did you quit?"

A shadow fell across his face. Tess felt the tension in his arm. He had taboo subjects just as she did.

"My heart went out of the game. When I first started, I told myself I would quit while

I was on top, so I did."

"What happened?"

For a long, breath-held moment Mac didn't say anything. The stark expression on his face conveyed the struggle he was having concerning what to tell her. She knew what it was like to have a past that haunted you. She reached out to place her hand on his arm to impart her support. He spoke in a low, barely audible voice.

"We were in the playoffs, and the score was tight. My wife went into labor early. No one told me until the game was over. By the time I got there, she was in surgery. I never got to say goodbye. I was too late."

"I'm sorry," she mumbled, knowing how inadequate those words really were. Beneath her hand his arm muscles bunched.

"I just couldn't play football after that."

"No one told you?"

"The game wasn't here in Denver, but that hour would have made a difference. The coach didn't realize that."

"I know how important it is to say goodbye. When you can't, you feel there's unfinished business between you."

His gaze swung to hers. "Have you lost someone close? Not been able to say goodbye?"

"Yes, my father had a heart attack. He

was fine one day. The next he was gone. My mother pined away and died within a year. They were so much in love she just didn't want to go on without him."

"How old were you?"

"Eighteen. My parents were older when they finally had me. They had tried to have children for years. I was a surprise, because they had given up. I think by the time I came along I was an intrusion." The second Tess said the last sentence she wanted to snatch it back. She had never voiced that thought to another human being. She hadn't allowed herself to think it because the implication hurt.

He brought her close to him, his hand massaging her arm. Silence reigned in the hospital room, only the occasional sounds from the hallway intruding. Tess laid her head on his shoulder and thought about what she had told him. In a short time he had learned more about her than most people she'd known for years knew. That in itself should warn her to stay as far away from the man as possible. Before long she would be telling him about Kevin and reliving those painful memories when all she wanted to do was forget and maybe in the process forgive herself.

In the dim light Mac shifted on the couch,

stretching his long legs in front of him. The feel of him next to her comforted her. Tess nestled closer to him, her eyelids drooping as the exhaustion she'd held at bay took over and sleep descended.

The scent of sandalwood washed over Tess, teasing her senses. Then she noticed that her body ached. Her face was pressed into something hard, angular. Her eyes snapped open to bright sunlight streaming through the slits in the blinds and forming stripes across the linoleum floor and the hospital bed that held Johnny.

Blinking, she straightened, her actions awakening the man next to her on the beige love seat. Her heartbeat began to race as his sleepy look took her in. She resisted the urge to brush a wayward lock of hair that had fallen onto his forehead. Much too intimate a gesture when she was trying desperately to keep this man at arm's length. One side of his mouth hitched up in a lopsided grin.

"Good morning, Tess."

The way he caressed her name caused her heart to beat even faster. She drew in a shallow breath, then a deeper one while she struggled to stand and put some space between them. She plowed her fingers through her hair and said, "I hadn't intended to fall asleep."

"You were tired." Mac leaned forward, resting his forearms on his thighs. "Besides, Johnny is here and still sound asleep."

She stared at the small boy in the bed, his features ashen, almost gaunt, and something twisted in her heart. She knew she couldn't save all the children, but what was it about this one that touched her so deeply? Kindred spirits? "I guess we weren't very good guards. Sleeping on the job."

"I'd better not add surveillance to my résumé, then."

His teasing comment eased the tension she'd experienced from waking up beside him on the couch. "I know it wasn't likely Johnny was going anywhere last night. He was very weak and dehydrated, but I just had to make sure."

"How about some coffee?"

"I don't want to leave yet."

"Then I'll go get us some and bring it back here."

"That would be great. I take cream and lots of sugar."

"How much is lots?"

"Four or five packets."

His eyes widened. "You drink hot sugar water with a little coffee flavor. You ruin a perfectly good drink."

"That's the only way I could drink coffee when I was younger. The habit has stuck with me. The coffee in the room behind the nurses' station is good. Get it there."

She watched him walk to the door and open it, a casual grace about his movements for such a large man. From what she had discovered about him on the playing field he had been surprisingly quick for his size. Not that she would ever tell him that she'd asked about him.

When he left, she stretched her arms above her head, then twisted from side to side to try to work the kinks from her body. She rarely slept sitting up and was surprised she had even though she was exhausted. But she could vividly recall the warmth and comfort she'd experienced when Mac's arm went about her shoulder and he held her close to him.

Out of the corner of her eye she saw Johnny move, trying to take the IV out. She rushed to his side and placed her hand over the connection. "If you think you're going somewhere, I have news for you, young man. You're staying put. Got that?" She schooled her voice into a no-nonsense tone, making sure he didn't hear the fear behind her words. Johnny was smart enough to use that.

The corners of his mouth turned down in a pout, and he glared at her.

She hovered over him like a mother hen protecting her young chick. "Understand?"

"Guess so," he mumbled and looked away.

Tess pulled the one hard-backed chair in the room to his bed and sat. "Good. I lost three nights of sleep because of you, and I don't know if I can keep that up. People count on me to be sharp when I work."

He turned his head to stare at her. "You did? Why?"

She gentled her stern expression. Johnny really didn't understand that she cared about him. She could see it in his confused look. "Because you're important to me. I care what happens to you. Why did you run away?"

"I ain't gonna stay with strangers. I can take care of myself."

She wanted to hug him to her and knew he would be upset if she tried. "With luck Mrs. Hocks will find a relative soon, and you won't have to stay with any strangers."

He huffed, his glare back. "I don't have no relatives I know. My grandma died a while back, and she was all there was."

Tess leaned forward. "Please promise me you won't run away again."

He clamped his lips together, his eyes narrow, his mouth set in a frown.

"Johnny?"

"I ain't gonna promise something I can't keep. My word is important to me."

"A man of his word. That's a good trait to have in life, Johnny."

Both Tess and Johnny glanced at Mac who stood at the end of the bed. She'd been so intent on the child she hadn't heard Mac enter the room. He smiled at her and held up a cup.

Taking a sip of the coffee, she welcomed the warm, sweet brew as it slid down her throat. She needed the time to compose a response to Johnny's declaration. "What if we can find someone you know to stay with?" she asked, desperate to keep him from running away, but not really sure how she could.

"Maybe." Johnny dropped his gaze from Mac who came around the bed to stand next to Tess.

"I'll have a word with Mrs. Hocks. I might be able to work something out." Tess toyed with the idea of taking care of Johnny but still didn't think that would be the best solution. He needed a family. He needed someone who would be there for him.

Johnny pulled the white sheet to his neck

and turned slightly on his side away from Tess. Mac nodded toward the door, and she rose. In the hallway Mac stopped her with his words. "I'll have a word with Mrs. Hocks about taking care of Johnny until she finds a permanent home for him."

Tess whirled. "You're a stranger. That won't work any better than the foster parents he ran away from."

"Since the nurse at the desk told me Johnny would be staying a few days in the hospital, I'll make it a point to get to know him."

"Just like that?" She snapped her fingers, not sure why she was upset by his solution. No, correction. She knew why. In order to get to know Johnny, Mac would have to visit him a lot at the hospital, and she was working the next few days, which meant she would see Mac a lot more than she wanted to.

He stepped closer. "Yes, just like that."

"He's a tough one to crack."

"I know that."

"Then how do you plan on doing it?"

"By being here for him. I'm not easily discouraged."

Another appealing quality about him, Tess thought, and wished she could find reasons not to like the man. "I need to go home and change. I'm on duty in less than an hour."

Mac headed for Johnny's room.

"What are you doing?"

"Getting started on getting acquainted with Johnny. See you in a while." He opened the door.

"Mac!"

His gaze found hers.

"Thanks for helping last night."

His smile lit his eyes. "Any time."

When Mac disappeared inside Johnny's room, Tess inhaled a deep, cleansing breath. Her legs felt like jelly, and her hands trembled. Exhaustion, she told herself, but that really wasn't the truth. Peter MacPherson affected her on many levels. Somehow over the next few days she was going to have to get real good at avoiding the man, because every time she was around him she felt herself weakening and dreaming of much more than friendship.

Chapter Six

You would think this pediatric floor would be big enough for the both of them, Tess thought, not for the first time that day. She fixed a polite smile on her face and said, "Johnny shouldn't be gone too much longer, Mac." Go find something to do that is useful. Quit driving me crazy. She wanted to add the words but remained silent, proud of herself.

"Do you think he'll like this?" Mac placed the handheld video game on the counter in front of her.

"Are you using bribery to win him over?"

"I'll use any means I need to in order to keep him off the streets." Mac slipped the game into the pocket of his navy blue windbreaker.

"You could regale him with some stories of your days playing football. The other kids seem to enjoy them."

"I've done that. It didn't work, and he leaves tomorrow. I asked Mrs. Hocks not to let him know just yet that I'd be his new foster parent."

"Chicken," she teased, not daring to let the man know how elated she was about him being Johnny's foster parent. Mac's family and home would be perfect for the child if Johnny would allow anyone through his tough shell.

Mac propped himself against the counter as though he was staying for awhile. "Okay, any bright ideas?"

Shaking her head, she laughed. "No, the video game is great. I haven't found a boy who doesn't like them." She glanced toward an orderly who was wheeling a patient down the hall. "And you'll get your chance right now to see what Johnny thinks. I have to get back to work before they fire me."

"They wouldn't do that. You're too valuable. I've seen you work with the kids. You're a natural," Mac said as he headed toward Johnny's room.

Tess really tried not to feel pleased by his compliment. That would only endear the man more to her, but his words warmed her. *You're a natural.* She repeated his words in her mind, her heart constricting. Memories of the times she and Kevin had discussed the family they were going to have inundated her, and for a moment she was flung back in time. She gripped the counter and closed her eyes, trying to right her world.

She forced herself to concentrate on her job. She had several temperatures that needed to be taken, then some notes to jot down. Work had been what had gotten her through the rough times before. And it would again, she told herself as she made her way toward a patient's room.

Half an hour later she stopped by the counter to grab a chart and saw Mac leaving Johnny's room, a frown etched into his features. Avoid him. She could have slipped into the examination room next to the nurses' station and gone unseen by Mac.

Instead, she walked up to him and said, "The video game didn't work."

"So much for your theory. He acted like he'd never seen one."

"Maybe he hasn't. He's never had much. What are you going to do now?"

"Try something else. I'm not giving up."

"What?"

He raked his hand through his hair, a frustrated expression on his face. "That's the problem. I'm fresh out of ideas."

"You were a boy once. What would you have liked?"

He thought a moment then his face brightened with a smile. "That's it! Thank you, Tess." He clasped her by the upper arms, drew her close and quickly planted a kiss on her cheek before hurrying away.

Tess stood in the middle of the busy hallway, stunned, her fingers caressing the place where his mouth had touched her skin briefly. She could swear it tingled. Beneath her hand she could feel the warmth of her blush as she thought of his kiss. Oh, my, what would she had done if he had kissed her on the mouth? Fainted?

Perplexed, Tess frowned. Why would Mac bring Amy to visit Johnny? Not ten minutes before, the two of them had disappeared into the boy's room. This was Mac's big idea to win Johnny over? Okay, maybe he knew something she didn't. He'd been a boy once. But a three-year-old girl?

Finally, after ten more minutes had passed and no one had left Johnny's room, Tess decided she couldn't wait any longer. She headed toward the door. Okay, so she needed lessons in how to avoid a man, but she was dying to see why he had brought Amy to visit Johnny. Usually a patient woman, she had to acknowledge she had no patience where Mac was concerned.

She pushed open the door and heard children's laughter spicing the air with warmth.

The sound wiped the frown from her face and lifted her spirits. Maybe the man knew what he was doing, after all. She stopped inside the room and took in the scene before her. Amy sat on the bed with Johnny, listening intently to him as he read a Dr. Seuss story about green eggs and ham.

Johnny finished the book and flipped it closed, setting it on his lap. He peered at Amy, a smile on his pale face. "I forgot how funny that story was."

"Daddy, I want green eggs 'morrow." Amy turned the book over and opened it. "Again — please."

She looked at Johnny, her big brown eyes framed by long, dark eyelashes, and Tess figured the little girl had made a conquest. Johnny wouldn't be able to resist that sweet, innocent face or those dimples in her plump cheeks as she smiled at him.

Johnny sighed heavily. "Okay. But only one more time."

Amy clapped. "Oh, goody. You do such a good job."

While Johnny started the story again, Mac slipped out of the chair and took Tess's arm to guide her from the room. "Is there something wrong?"

She shook her head. "No, it looks like you have everything under control. But I don't understand why you brought Amy here."

"Once when I was about eleven I was in the hospital because my appendix had to be removed. The one thing that made me feel better was seeing my family — even my sisters. Little children have a way of making a person forget about his troubles. I was hurting but I didn't care. I put on a front for them, and before long, I forgot about my own pain and enjoyed their company. I thought Amy could help Johnny."

"I don't believe it. It's working."

"It's a start. She brought her favorite book to share with him, and when she asked him to read it, he couldn't say no even though I know he wanted to."

"How many times has he read it?"

"Three. Actually Amy could recite it for Johnny, but the last time he started using different voices for the characters, and she loved that. I don't quite get into the story like he did."

She cocked her head. "And why not?"

"Because I've read that book probably three hundred times. After the first twenty times it kinda loses its appeal."

She chuckled. "I can see what you mean."

"I'd better get back inside. Amy can overstay her welcome. I want to win him over, not chase him away. Oh, by the way, Casey

116

starts work here tomorrow."

"Good," Tess said and wanted to groan. Another MacPherson in her life. At this rate she would never be rid of the man.

After Mac and Amy left, Tess paid another visit to Johnny. He plucked at the sheet, his gaze fixed on his lap, his forehead wrinkled in deep thought. He didn't even look up when she entered the room.

"Amy's quite a character," Tess said.

"She's okay for a girl," Johnny mumbled, his head still down, his hands twisting the sheet.

"I know she enjoyed you reading that story to her."

"Yeah, I guess so." Finally Johnny looked up. "Why did Mr. MacPherson bring his daughter to see me?"

"He's taken an interest in you."

"Well, I don't need no one to care."

Tess straightened the bedding, needing something to do with her hands. The urge to pull the child into her arms was so strong she was afraid she would act on it and really upset Johnny. He wasn't ready for that. She didn't know if he ever would be. The shell about his heart was tougher than hers.

"Do you know what Amy said to me? She said she had lots of cousins but no brothers and sisters. She wants a brother and sister, but she knows her dad doesn't like to talk about it."

"Is that right?" Tess's hands trembled as she fluffed his pillows.

"She says her mommy is in heaven watching over her. She told me mine was doing the same thing."

"She's right."

"Then why isn't my mother doing a good job?"

The question caught Tess off guard. She didn't have an answer for the child. Why did children like Johnny suffer? There was a time when she would have readily been able to answer him. Now her doubts about the Lord plagued her and made her wonder why, too.

She pasted a bright smile on her face and said, "I know, Johnny, you'll get better. I know that in here." She pressed her hand over her heart, fighting the tears clogging her throat. "Everything will work out." She had to believe that. She didn't want to give the child false hope, but neither could she tell him that bad things happened to good people.

"Sure. You have to say that." He turned and presented his back to her.

She reached out toward Johnny, wanting to connect with him, but she knew he would reject any attempt on her part to touch him. "No, Johnny, I don't have to say anything," she murmured and left the room. She hoped that somehow Mac could reach this child, because she couldn't seem to.

"May I join you?"

Tess glanced up to find Casey standing beside her table with a lunch tray in her hands. The young woman wore a hopeful expression on her face, and Tess could remember her first day on the job. So much to learn, so many new people.

"Of course." After Mac's sister sat, Tess asked, "How's the job so far?"

"Great. A bit overwhelming, but then I expected that since it's a new job." Casey popped a French fry, smothered in ketchup, into her mouth. "I was supposed to meet Mac here for lunch, but I guess he's running late. He wanted to get everything ready for Johnny."

"When's he going to tell Johnny?"

"This afternoon when Mrs. Hocks visits." Casey took a bite of her hamburger, chewed it quickly, then leaned forward and said, "I'm so glad he's decided to do this. Being a foster parent will be good for Mac. He's great with children. He wanted a whole bunch of them with Sheila."

The aroma of onions and hamburger made Tess wish she had gotten what Mac's sister was eating. Tomato soup and tossed green salad were good for her diet but didn't do much for her appetite. "Well, he's still young."

With a frown Casey munched on another fry. "I don't know. When his wife died, something happened to Mac. He doesn't talk about it, but he took her death especially hard. I think —"

"Casey, I see you couldn't wait for me to eat lunch." Mac swung into the chair between his sister and Tess.

Tess tamped down the disappointment she was experiencing at Mac's untimely interruption. Everyone was so guarded about Mac and his relationship with his deceased wife. On the outside it appeared as though he had moved on, but Tess got the feeling that really wasn't the case. He was still dealing with her death as Tess was with Kevin's.

"You're late. I have a schedule to maintain now."

"Sorry. Traffic. I had to sign some more papers at Mrs. Hocks's office." Mac shifted his attention to Tess. "How's Johnny today?"

"Not saying much, which really isn't that unusual."

"Well, now that I have everything signed, sealed and delivered, I'm gonna tell him about the arrangement I have with Mrs. Hocks."

"Good luck." Tess looked around. "Where's Amy? I thought you might bring reinforcements today to help bolster your case."

Mac chuckled. "If this is gonna work with Johnny, he'll have to accept me. We might as well see how receptive he is to the idea of me being his foster parent."

"Besides, this is Mom's day with Amy, and nothing interferes with that. You can't get Mom near a hospital," Casey added, stuffing another French fry into her mouth.

"Do you want moral support when you tell him?" Tess asked, trying to ignore her mouth watering at the quickly disappearing fries on Casey's plate.

His eyes crinkled at the corners, a smile deep in their depths. "I'd love it."

"Then let me know, and I'll try to be there."

"How about now?"

"Fine. I have fifteen more minutes of my lunch break." After downing the last few swallows of her iced tea, Tess rose.

"You guys gonna leave me to eat alone?"

"Casey, if I know you, you'll have a whole flock of people around you in no time." Mac picked up Tess's tray to place on the conveyor belt near the exit. "I'll stop by and see you after I talk with Johnny."

Tess saw the nervous smile Mac sent his sister and knew he was concerned about this meeting. She took his hand in hers and said, "Kids can tell when someone cares. That's gonna mean something to Johnny."

"Will you come to dinner tonight?"

Tess blinked, surprised by the invitation. Words of refusal lodged in her throat.

"I could use your support during his first night with the family. A familiar face will help."

She choked back her refusal and nodded. Releasing his grasp before she became too comfortable holding his hand, she went through the swinging cafeteria doors and headed for the bank of elevators.

On the ride to the pediatric floor Mac lounged against the stainless-steel wall with his arms crossed over his chest. "What time do you get off work?"

"Three."

"You could follow us home."

"I rode with Delise."

"Then you can ride with us, and I'll take you home later tonight. We'll have an early dinner since I'm sure Johnny will be tired his first day out of the hospital."

"How are you going to prevent him from running away?"

Pushing away from the wall, Mac prepared to exit the elevator as it came to a stop. "If he wants to, short of locking him in his room, I can't. All I can do is show him I care about him and make him a part of my family."

"I hope that's enough." Remembering how pale and drawn the child had been after his last bout on the street, Tess chewed her bottom lip, worried that no one would be able to stop Johnny from running away again.

When they reached the child's room, Tess hung back, realizing Mac would have to be the one to convince Johnny he wanted to be his foster parent. The boy saw both of them, slipped the video game under the top sheet and frowned at them.

"Did you want something?"

Mac pulled the hard chair close to the bed. "To talk."

"What about?" Johnny narrowed his eyes on Mac.

Mac inhaled a deep breath and said, "About you coming to stay with me and Amy."

Johnny's gaze widened for a few seconds, then slid from Mac's face. "Stay with you?"

"I have plenty of room. In fact, my house is too big for just Amy and me. We were hoping you'd share it with us." When Johnny remained quiet, Mac added, "Mrs. Hocks has given her okay. You have to stay with someone. I'd like it to be us."

Tess watched Johnny ball the white sheet in his hands, the video game slipping off his lap. It would have fallen to the floor if Mac hadn't been quick and caught it in midair. Mac didn't say a word to Johnny about the game, just set it on the child's lap, his gaze fixed on Johnny.

The child latched onto the video game, his grip tight. "Okay, for the time being."

"Great! I'm gonna make the arrangements, then I'll be back to pick you up. Tess is going home with us after her shift is over at three. I need to call Amy and tell her you're coming. She's so excited."

"She is?"

"She told me not to come home without you."

Johnny stared wide-eyed at Mac as he left the room, his hands clenched around the video game so tight that his knuckles were white. "Did you ask him to do this?"

"No, he came up with the idea all on his

own. I think it's a good idea."

"It's only temporary."

Tess's heart ached. She came to sit where Mac had been and took Johnny's hand. She felt his tremor as he curled his fingers into a ball. "We don't know what the future holds for us. Things will work out," she said with more conviction than she really felt.

Johnny gripped her for a few seconds before he realized it and released his grasp. "Yeah, they always do," he mumbled.

Tess hated to hear sarcasm in such a young child. He was world-weary and only ten years old.

"We're home," Mac called as he stepped into his house with Johnny and Tess beside him.

Amy came running from the den and flung herself into Mac's arms. He picked her up and planted a big kiss on her cheek.

"Look who I brought home, pumpkin." Mac put Amy down.

The little girl swung her attention to Johnny and smiled. "Good. I want to show you my toys." She took his hand and started for her bedroom. "Daddy said we can get a puppy."

"Daddy said we will talk about it," Mac replied to the two retreating backs. He turned to Tess with a helpless expression on his face.

She shrugged. "Don't look at me. Personally I think a dog would be great. I wish I could have one in my apartment."

"You don't have to convince me. I've left it up to Nina. She'll be the one cleaning up its messes."

"And I haven't decided." Nina walked into the foyer, wiping her hands on her apron. "Where's Johnny? Did I miss him?"

"Amy's already captured him and dragged him to her room to show off her doll collection."

"Something I'm sure the boy is dying to see. I'd better go rescue the child." Nina headed for the hallway that led to the bedrooms.

"Come on. Let's go into the den. It won't be long before Nina brings them in there."

"How long has she worked for you?"

"Before I was married, and since Amy's birth she lives here. I don't know what I would have done without her help. She's priceless and she knows it."

Just as Mac predicted, Nina brought the two children into the den a few minutes later. From the expression on Johnny's face Tess realized the boy was probably shell-shocked. Amy was still chattering as they walked into the room.

When Amy saw her father, she went up to him and asked, "When can we go pick out a puppy? I told Johnny he could name her."

"A her, is it?"

"Yes, so she can have puppies."

"You have this all figured out?"

Amy nodded.

Mac looked at Nina. "What do you think?"

"I think this weekend would be a good time," the housekeeper answered.

"You heard Nina. We'll get a puppy this weekend."

Smiling from ear to ear, Amy turned to Tess. "Will you come, too?"

"Well —" Tess searched her mind for a reason to say no, but she couldn't come up with one, especially when several pairs of eyes were glued to her waiting for her answer. "Fine. What time on Saturday?"

"I thought we would go out to Colt's farm after church on Sunday. Why don't you go with us to church? We can make it an all-day outing."

Tess glanced at Amy then Johnny and couldn't refuse, even though the outing was turning into something she wasn't ready to deal with. "Okay," she answered slowly, feeling as though she'd been cornered.

"Good. Church begins at nine-thirty. I'd better warn you. The whole MacPherson clan will be at church."

"Whoa. I'm not sure I remember everyone's name."

"That's okay. I'll help you," Amy said, climbing into her father's lap.

"How many are there?" Johnny asked, his eyes round.

"Too many to count. We'll just have to stick together on Sunday, Johnny."

"Tess. Tess," Mac said, shaking his head, "don't scare the child away. I know my family can be a bit overwhelming, but there are only thirty or thirty-five of them."

"Thirty? Thirty-five? You don't know how many people are in your family?"

"Well, it depends on what you want to classify as family. I have a few first cousins you haven't met yet. And then there are my second and third cousins."

Tess raised a hand to stop him. "That's enough. I'll never keep everyone straight. I have a terrible time with people's names. Faces I can remember. Names go in one ear and out the other."

Mac grinned. "I'll help, too. And, Johnny, my large family just means you have a lot of children to play with. My family's looking forward to meeting you."

"They are?" Johnny squeaked, a bit over-whelmed, a stunned expression on his face.

"Come on, pumpkin. Let's show Johnny his bedroom. You look like you could rest before we have dinner." Mac rose and set his daughter on the floor.

When Johnny stood in the doorway of his room, he scanned the area that had obviously been decorated with a boy in mind. There was a blue bedspread on the double bed and a few toys on top of it. A computer sat on the desk with a fish tank on a stand next to it. The light illuminated several angelfish and some other types of fish for which Tess didn't know the names.

"This is for me?" the boy said in awe, taking a few steps into the room and slowly turning in a full circle.

"I didn't want to do too much. You can hang whatever posters you want." Mac settled his hand on the boy's shoulder. "Go on and make yourself at home."

Johnny walked to the navy blue beanbag in the corner and sat in it, bouncing a few times. Next to it was a bookcase with books on two shelves. He perused the titles. "The Hardy Boys?"

"I know those books are old. They were mine when I was growing up. We can get you some books that you like to read. Amy and I go to the library once a week. I hope you'll join us."

Johnny didn't say anything. He just stared at the Hardy Boys mysteries on the shelf next to him, running his finger along the spines of several to them.

"I think it would be a good idea if you rested for a while," Tess said, noting the dark circles under Johnny's eyes and the ashen cast to his skin.

Tess knew he was feeling tired when he didn't protest but lay down on the bed and closed his eyes. Everyone backed out of the room, and Mac quietly closed the door.

"Do you want to see my room?" Amy asked, taking Tess's hand and guiding her toward the door next to Johnny's.

"I'd be honored."

"While Amy shows you her room, I'm gonna help Nina get dinner ready. Come into the kitchen when you're through with the tour."

As Tess crossed the threshold into the little girl's bedroom, she glanced at Mac disappearing down the hall. He stopped at the end and peered back. The smile that lit his face melted her insides, and she knew she was in big trouble. He was even more appealing on his home turf.

Chapter Seven

Tess held Amy and Johnny's hands as they left the sanctuary. She sensed Mac behind her with members of his family flanking him. Alice grasped Amy's other hand. The mass of people leaving the church slowed as they approached the pastor and stopped to say a few words to him.

Pastor Winthrop's message still rang through Tess's mind. "Wherefore I say unto you, All manner of sin and blasphemy shall be forgiven unto men; but the blasphemy against the Holy Ghost shall not be forgiven unto men." The Bible verse from Matthew described the power of the Lord's forgiveness. Then why couldn't she forgive herself for surviving and continuing to live after so many of the people she'd cared about had died?

When she laughed, she thought of Jorge, who would never be able to tell her one of his silly jokes again. When she helped a patient, she thought of Kevin, who had devoted his life to the Lord and medicine, feeling the power of both could do anything . . . except save his life.

The family ahead of them moved on, and Tess came face to face with Pastor Winthrop. Her hand trembled as she reached out to shake his and say, "Your sermon was thought-provoking."

"Good. That's what I want to do. Get my congregation thinking about the Lord."

"I'm Tess Morgan, a friend of Mac's. I'm just visiting for the day."

"I hope you'll come back. We always love to have new faces around here. Alice is a great one for recruiting people to help with various tasks that need to be done at the church. Don't be surprised if she calls you up. Before long, you might become a regular."

Mac's mother laughed. "Now, Pastor Winthrop, I'm not that bad. But I do run a tight ship where the Lord is concerned. His house must be kept tidy."

"And I for one appreciate all your efforts."

Mac leaned forward. "You ought to see what she has planned for the spring festival."

"Speaking of which, I need to talk to you about some of the plans." Alice stood to the side to allow her large family to file by while she remained to speak with the pastor.

"Tess, let's get everyone into the car. We have about an hour's drive to Colt's farm." Mac touched the small of her back.

"Who is this Colt?"

"He was a teammate of mine, a few years behind me. When he retired a year after I did, he bought himself a farm and takes in stray animals."

"I thought you were going to get a puppy."

"He has several puppies, but he also has other dogs that need a home."

"Be careful. You might come home with more than one." Casey came up behind them, clasping her brother on the shoulder. "You were always a sucker for a stray animal."

"I'm not the one who adopted a baby squirrel, a robin and a fox, and that wasn't that long ago."

"You know, come to think of it I would like to ride out there with you."

"And do what, young lady?" Alice said, joining the small group.

"We don't have a dog. I think it's about time we got another one."

"That's what I was afraid you thought." Alice turned to Mac. "Don't let her bring home anything bigger than Amy."

"Then I can get a dog, too?" Casey asked, surprise evident in her expression.

"With our growing family, it would be nice to have a dog for the children to play with when they come over. Did you hear the news? Kayla is pregnant. With Mary due in a few months that'll make two babies born this year to the MacPhersons. Not a bad year, if I say so myself."

Mac saw Kayla with her husband, Paul. He swept his sister up and swung her around. "Way to go, Kayla. Your patience has finally paid off."

"I gather Mother told you the news."

Tess hung back as the members of Kayla's family congratulated her. Tess held Johnny's hand, but Amy was in the midst of the adults in her father's arms, joining in the festive activities. Mac glanced at Tess and Johnny and stepped away from the group. He took Tess's arm and pulled her and Johnny into the family.

"I know that we arrived late so I didn't get to make the introductions. This is Johnny. He'll be staying with me and Amy. Some of you have already met Tess at Steve's birthday party."

Mac went around the group surrounding them, giving each person's name and the relationship to him. By the time he had finished, the spacious foyer of the church was filled with thirty members of Mac's family. Johnny yanked on Tess's arm, and she leaned down for him to whisper into her ear.

"Am I supposed to remember all these people?"

"No one expects you to. Now, me, they probably do. I'll let you in on a secret. My mind stopped at the sixth name. We'll work on it together."

"It probably won't make any difference. I won't be here that long."

She saw the corners of the child's mouth twist down in a frown. "Why do you say that?"

"Because it's the truth. I have no home. Since my mother died, I never stay long in any one place." Johnny sidestepped, the look on his face discouraging further discussion.

Tess still feared that Johnny would run away. She hoped that wasn't what he meant and realized she would have to let Mac know what Johnny had told her. She wanted this situation to work for everyone, because Mrs. Hocks wasn't optimistic that she would locate any of Johnny's relatives willing to take a ten-year-old boy.

As the members of Mac's family moved

slowly toward the double brass doors that led outside, Tess peered at the entrance to the sanctuary. There was a time when she would have gone into the church and prayed to God to keep Johnny safe and to find a home for him. Now she was afraid to ask — wasn't sure how to. Her prayers before hadn't worked.

"We'd better leave for the farm if we want to get home by dark," Mac said at her side.

She glanced at him. Mac glowed with self-confidence. In that moment she felt everything would work out just as she had told Johnny it would. "Lead the way."

Mac waved his goodbyes to the rest of his family. "Casey, you hop in back with Amy and Johnny and behave yourself."

"Me? I'm always good on road trips."

"Don't get me started on that one." Mac opened the door to the passenger's side for Tess. "Remind me to tell you later about our family trip to the Grand Canyon."

"That's not fair. I was only four at the time."

"She started out by getting sick all over me."

"If you get car sick, you can sit up front." Tess twisted to add, "I don't mind riding in the back."

Mac laughed. "She didn't get sick be-

136

cause she was riding in the car. She got sick because she ate a whole box of chocolate candy an hour before we left."

"A whole box!" Johnny buckled his seat belt.

"To this day I can't eat chocolate. It makes my stomach churn."

"That's awful. I can't imagine not liking chocolate."

"So, Johnny, you're a big fan of chocolate, are you?" Mac pulled out of the parking lot.

"Any way I can get it."

"Then you're gonna fit right in. Amy and I love chocolate. How about you, Tess?"

"Yep, I have to say I have a hard time passing it up."

"Okay, you guys, if you're trying to make me feel left out, you're doing a great job."

"Never, Aunt Casey. I love you." Amy threw her arms around Casey and gave her a hug.

"I love you, too, squirt," Casey said, tickling the little girl in her side.

Tess settled back, listening to the giggles and laughter. Before long Johnny was drawn into the fun with Amy and Casey ganging up on him. The three only calmed down when Mac threatened to stop the car in the middle of the highway.

"Casey Leigh MacPherson, I knew it was a mistake to bring you. Contain yourself for the children's sake." Mac's amused tone belied his words.

"Aye, aye, sir. Just as soon as I thoroughly orient Johnny to the Tickle Monster."

Another burst of laughter sounded in the car, prompting Tess to smile and say, "I think your sister is a lost cause."

"One of my many burdens," Mac said with an exaggerated sigh.

"Thank goodness we aren't too far from the farm."

"Uncle, uncle," Johnny called between giggles.

"I think he's thoroughly oriented, Mac." Casey sat between the children as though she hadn't caused a major upheaval in the car, her back straight, her hands clasped together in her lap, an innocent expression on her face.

"Now I'll get a good night's sleep." Mac's gaze twinkled as it found Tess's for a brief moment before he returned his attention to the highway.

His look continued to undermine her determination to keep an emotional distance from Peter MacPherson. Tess focused on the beautiful mountainous terrain and tried not to think of the man next to her or the at-

138

mosphere of camaraderie that abounded in the car. Its lure tore at the barriers she'd erected around her heart, making her think of all kinds of possibilities.

Thirty minutes later Mac turned off the highway onto a dirt road that led to a log cabin set at the base of a mountain and nestled in a grove of pine trees. Tess counted five dogs and three cats in the yard as he brought the car to a stop in front of the house. A huge man, taller and bigger than Mac, came onto the porch and waved.

"What was Colt's position on the team?" Tess asked, staring at the man who made Mac look small.

"Tackle. He's six-seven and weighs three hundred fifty pounds. He prides himself on saying it's all muscles."

"Oh, my," Casey whispered from the back while Colt left his porch and approached the car.

"Good to see you, Mac. Glad to see your leg has finally mended," Colt said as everyone climbed out of the vehicle.

Mac shook Colt's hand, then gestured toward the group behind him. "You know Amy."

"She's looking more and more like Sheila every time I see her."

"That's what Daddy says. I'm the spittin'

—" Amy screwed her face into a thoughtful expression. "Spittin'?"

"Image, pumpkin."

"Yeah." Amy craned her neck and grinned at Colt. "You're tall."

"And this is Tess, Casey, my sister, and Johnny." Mac pointed to each person.

"Well, you all are in luck. I have a nice selection of puppies for you to look at." Colt began walking toward a barn about a hundred yards from his log cabin. "I hope you'll stay for lunch."

Tess scanned the barn, the scent of hay and animals filling the air. Along one side were stalls, all empty except one with a horse in it. Various pens were along the opposite wall with rabbits, a coyote and a hawk in them. A calico cat came up to Tess and rubbed its body along her leg before ambling over to Colt, who picked it up and stroked it, its purring added to the other noises the animals were making.

The children were drawn to a pen with six mixed-breed puppies waddling around. They were brown and black, and two of them were fighting over an old slipper. One nudged its nose under the bedding until it had managed to trap itself. It couldn't figure out how to get out. Colt stepped over the wire fencing and rescued the puppy.

"Can I hold her?" Casey asked, climbing into the pen.

"Me, too, Aunt Casey."

Tess noticed Johnny leaning over the fence and petting the runt of the litter. "Go on and pick her up."

Johnny threw her a look of uncertainty, straightening immediately as though caught doing something wrong. "I might drop her."

Tess reached into the pen and lifted the runt out, thrusting the puppy into his arms. "No, you won't."

The boy hesitantly took the squirming puppy from Tess and held it close to his chest. She began to chew on his finger, content in Johnny's arms.

"I may have a problem here," Mac said, coming up behind Tess.

"What?"

"Look at Amy and Johnny. Both are falling in love with different puppies."

"You could always get both of them."

"And have Nina walk out on me? How would I ever survive without her?"

"I suspect Nina can be won over. I think she'll take one look at Johnny and Amy with their puppies and won't say a word."

"I like your optimism. If she says anything, I'll tell her you assured me she would be okay with it."

"Daddy. Daddy, I want this one." Amy picked her way through the rambunctious puppies and held hers up for him to look at.

Johnny's grin of delight vanished, and he put his runt in the pen, then shifted away from the fence. Tess's heart twisted at the closed expression descending on his boyish face, the hunched shoulders and folded arms.

"How about if we pick two? Which one would you like, Johnny?"

Mac turned toward the child, whose chin rested on his chest.

Johnny's head came up, and his eyes brightened. "You want me to choose one, too?"

"Sure. The puppy will be your responsibility if you want it."

"I —" Johnny gulped. "Yes."

Mac retrieved the runt from the pen and handed it to Johnny. "Is this the one you want?"

"Yes." The boy buried his face in the puppy's fur, rubbing his cheek against her. His grin was ear to ear.

"We get two puppies! Neat, Daddy. Then Johnny can name his and I can name mine." Amy cradled hers in her arms. "I think I'll call her Buttons."

Mac lifted his daughter out of the pen while she still held her puppy. "But both of you have to feed them and make sure they have enough exercise."

"I will," Johnny and Amy said, almost at the same time.

"Well, now that is out of the way, let's go up to the house. I have some stew on the stove. I hope you guys brought your appetites. I don't get to cook often for guests and I think I went overboard."

Everyone filed out of the barn, the two puppies left in their pen until later. Tess paused outside the large double doors and took a deep breath of the mountain air, perfumed with the scent of spring. The sun warmed her face while a light breeze blew strands of her hair as though dancing on it.

"I always enjoy visiting Colt. Sometimes I wished I'd moved up here, away from the hustle and bustle of Denver."

"Why didn't you?" Tess asked, slanting a look at Mac who stopped next to her while the rest headed for the log cabin.

"One word, family. They depend on me, and this is just too far away."

Tess would have given anything to be able to say that. She'd wanted a large family, and now that didn't seem a possibility. Her dream had died on that mountaintop in

South America as surely as Kevin had, but that didn't stop her from wishing.

"And then, of course, there's the halfway house I volunteer at and the foundation I run. I suppose I could manage to run the foundation if I lived here, but I wouldn't particularly like commuting to Denver and I can't see giving up my work at the halfway house."

"That's important to you?"

"Very. A lot of the people I work with have lost hope. I try to give them their hope back."

"How?" She wanted hers back, but didn't know how to go about finding it.

"Through the Lord, Tess."

"What if the Lord took your hope away?"

"Only you can do that for yourself." He stood in front of her, blocking her view of the log cabin. Taking both her hands in his, he continued, "Let me help you, Tess. I know you're hurting. I'm a good listener."

His words tempted her to tell all, to open up the wounds and bleed again. Maybe then she would heal. Where would she begin? Fear held the words inside.

"The Lord's a good listener. If not me, then talk to Him."

Tess yanked her hands from his. "I tried, and it didn't work." Her throat closed. Her

144

tears, which lately had been so close to the surface, threatened to flow again. She couldn't cry in front of Mac. She swallowed several times and said in as cheerful voice as possible, "I don't know about you, but I'm hungry." She stepped around him and hurried toward the cabin and people who wouldn't demand something of her she couldn't give.

"Tess," Mac called.

She didn't stop. At the door into the cabin, she glanced back and saw Mac standing where she'd left him. She thrust open the door and rushed inside, desiring to hear sounds of other people. The scent of baking bread, meat and onions saturated the air, making her feel welcome.

She paused a few feet inside the cabin and surveyed her surroundings. She felt as though she had stepped back in time. There was one large room with a massive fireplace along the back wall. The kitchen and dining areas were off to the side of the main room, and two doors that probably led to bedrooms were on the opposite side. The oak furniture was simple, sturdy and fit well into the rustic environment.

Casey and the children were setting the long table with enough benches for eight people to sit on. Johnny laughed at something Casey said while Amy tugged on Colt's pant leg. When he looked down at her, she indicated she wanted to be picked up so she could peek into the large black kettle on the stove.

The door behind Tess opened and closed. She felt Mac's presence, the air charged with his vitality the second he entered the cabin. Her heart reacted by increasing its beat, and her mouth went dry. The hairs on her neck tingled, and she knew he was staring at her, probably trying to figure out what made her tick.

"Daddy, Colt let me stir the stew and taste it to make sure it was ready for us to eat." Amy raced across the large room and tugged on Mac's arm to lead him to the group. "I'm gonna ask Nina if I can help her, too."

Tess heard Mac mutter as he passed her, "Nina is gonna be thrilled to hear that. I remember that last time you had more flour on you than in the bowl."

"Ah, Daddy, I was two then. I'm bigger now."

"That was only six months ago."

"Yeah, but I'm all grown up now." Amy straightened her small body, adding an inch to her height.

Tess hid her smile behind her hand while

Mac answered his daughter with a grunt that could mean just about anything.

Johnny spied her and said, "Tess, Colt has two new puppies that he has to feed himself. Someone left them on the highway. Come look." He waved her over to a cardboard box sitting in front of the fireplace. "They can't be more than a week old."

Tess looked inside at the two white balls curled together, sleeping on an old terrycloth towel. "They're lucky he found them. They wouldn't have made it on their own."

"Why do people discard animals like that?" Johnny said in a whisper as if he was afraid of waking up the puppies.

"I wish I had a good answer for you. Some people don't value life very much." She thought of the men who had invaded the mountain village, shooting at anything that moved.

"Come and get it. Lunch is being served," Colt announced.

"No one's gonna hurt Frisky. I'll make sure of that." Johnny straightened, a fierce expression on his face.

"Is Frisky the name of your puppy?"

He nodded, his hands clenched at his sides, while his gaze was riveted on the sleeping puppies. "She won't be the runt for long. I'll take real good care of her."

"Then that's all she can ask," Tess said to Johnny while they found a bench to sit on.

After everyone was served, Colt bowed his head and said, "Heavenly Lord, bless this food and watch out for the animals who need help. Send them to my door and I will provide. Amen."

"How many animals are you caring for right now?" Casey passed the basket of homemade bread to Colt, who sat next to her.

"Gosh, I'm not sure." He silently counted on his fingers, then announced, "Thirty-one if you excluded the two puppies you're taking back to Denver."

"Make that three. Except that Mom requested a dog, not a puppy." Casey lavished butter on her piece of bread. "Do you have any dogs that need homes?"

"I have seven you can choose from."

"The ride back home should be interesting. Five people and three animals." Mac shook his head as though he couldn't believe he had agreed to do this.

"What made you take in stray animals?" Tess asked, sipping her tall glass of iced water.

"It sorta just happened. One day someone dumped some puppies out on the highway. Then I found a stray cat that was pretty beaten up. The rest is history. People around here know that if they don't want an animal I'll take it in and try to find it a home. I think my reputation is spreading. Every week I get more and more. I'm gonna have to take on help if this pace keeps up."

"I want to help," Amy said after stuffing a spoonful of stew into her mouth.

"Me, too," Johnny chimed in.

"Hold it, kids. I think that would be great, but Colt lives too far away for that to be practical. Sorry." Mac handed his daughter a napkin to wipe her mouth.

"We gots to do somethin', Daddy."

"You are. You're taking in two puppies who need homes."

"But I want to do more."

"Sorry, pumpkin. It's not possible."

"Tell you what, guys. I'll bring you out here one Saturday, and if Colt doesn't mind, we can help him." Casey threw a smile toward the man in question.

"Mind? The more the merrier."

"When, Aunt Casey?"

"Soon. I need to check my schedule at the hospital."

"We could do it some other day."

"No, Amy. Johnny will be starting school next week." Mac took the last bite of his stew.

"School! I ain't going."

"That's not an option."

Johnny pouted. "I won't know nobody. Besides, I don't feel too well."

"The doctor told me you could start next week half days." Mac's features firmed into an expression that told the child this was a battle he wouldn't win.

Tess remembered the comment Johnny had made about not being long in any one place. She would definitely have to say something to Mac this evening so he would be aware of what Johnny was feeling. She hoped the child wouldn't do something drastic to avoid going to school.

"Well, I don't know about everyone else, but I'm ready for dessert." Colt rose and took his plate toward the sink.

"What is it?" Amy asked, her eyes growing round as Colt brought a plate with a top over it.

"Chocolate cake."

Casey groaned while the rest cheered.

"I think they both are finally asleep." Mac entered the den and sat across from Tess. "Johnny insisted his puppy stay in his room with him. Frisky is in the box, but I won't be surprised to find the puppy in bed with Johnny later on."

150

"Where's Amy's?"

"In the utility room."

"How did you get her to agree to part with Buttons? I thought they were attached from the time she got in the car with her."

"Not easily. Of course, when she finds out Johnny slept with Frisky, I'll have a problem on my hands."

"You couldn't say no to Johnny?"

Mac shook his head. "I tried honestly, but the boy has had so little in his life. All I could think of was how I felt about my first puppy, and the word yes just came out." He gave her a sheepish look. "I really do know how to draw the line. Honest."

"I believe you," Tess said with a laugh.

The grandfather clock in the corner chimed nine times. Tess glanced at it, surprised at how late it was. She had to get up early tomorrow and work, and yet she hadn't talked to Mac about what Johnny said. "Speaking of Johnny, he said something to me today that I think you should be aware of, Mac. It's probably nothing, but he said he wasn't going to be at your house long. Do you think he's planning anything?"

Frowning, Mac plowed his hand through his hair. "I hope Frisky will change that. If he feels responsible for her, he might think twice about running away."

151

"So that was your motive. Good plan."

"Actually my plan is to make him feel part of this family."

"What happens when he has to leave because Mrs. Hocks has found a relative to take him in?"

Mac's brow creased with a deep frown. "We don't know how long that'll be, if ever."

"That's true. Have you thought about all the possibilities?"

"Like what?"

"What if Mrs. Hocks never finds a relative, what then?"

"That's easy. I'll take care of Johnny."

"What if she does find someone? Are you prepared to let him go?"

Mac drew in a deep breath and released it slowly. "I'll have to. I've placed this in God's hands. This will work out for the best for Johnny."

"I sure hope so. The child has been through so much in his short ten years. He's so afraid to care."

"I know, Tess."

The look Mac gave her spoke of his concerns, which went deeper than Johnny's fear of getting close to another. Her own fears connected her to the child, and both she and Mac were aware of that. If only she

152

could turn her life over to the Lord, then maybe . . .

"I'd better get home. It's a long day tomorrow." Tess stood abruptly, needing to leave before she broke down and told Mac her life story. It was a boring subject she wanted to avoid. Spilling her guts wouldn't change what had happened.

"When will I get to see you again? How about coming to dinner one night this week?"

Tess bent and picked up her black purse, hoisting it on her shoulder. She was so tempted to accept his invitation, not just because she would be able to see Johnny. But she needed to toughen her resolve to put some emotional distance between her and — who was she kidding — Mac. "Not this week. Sorry. Extra busy."

"Well, then, I'll see you at the hospital."

"You will?" Her grip tightened on her purse strap. Why was he making it so hard to avoid him?

"I've worked out a visiting schedule with the child life specialist, Cindy. I should have done something like this sooner. I'm organizing some of my football buddies to help."

"Oh, that's good. The children will love that," Tess replied, aware the enthusiasm she should be feeling wasn't present in her voice even though she pasted a bright smile on her face.

"Cindy was excited about it." He escorted her toward the front door. "So I guess you'll just have to get used to me being in your life."

The twinkle in his eyes emphasized he knew exactly what she was trying to do and that he wasn't going to let her. Her smile faltered. "I'll wave to you while I'm working. Some days I'm so busy I don't even get a break."

Mac held the front door for her. "I'll be sure to wave back. Good night, Tess, and thank you for sharing your day with us. It meant a lot to —" he paused for a few seconds "— Johnny."

Tess felt Mac's gaze on her as she walked to her car, parked in his circular drive. Reaching to open her door, she noticed the quiver in her hand as it clasped the handle and pulled. He was deliberately undermining her resolve, and she wasn't going to let him get away with it. But as she slid behind the steering wheel, she wasn't sure how she was going to stop him.

Chapter Eight

Mac heard muffled voices then a giggle coming from Johnny's room. Pausing in the hallway, he listened. Thirty minutes before Amy had dashed through the den with a box, saying hi and bye all in the same breath. Then not ten minutes after that Johnny had hurried into the kitchen, retrieved a bowl and disappeared to his bedroom with not one word of greeting as he passed through the den. All this after they had put their puppies in the utility room. What were those two doing?

Mac knocked on Johnny's bedroom door, waited a few seconds, then pushed it open just in time to see the boy throw a blanket over the box, then sit with Amy in front of it. One look at the children's expressions told Mac everything he needed to know.

He fisted his hands on his hips. "Okay, what are you two hiding in that box?"

"Nothin', Daddy." Amy stuck her thumb into her mouth, a clear sign to Mac that she wasn't telling the truth.

He riveted his attention to the ten-year-old. "Johnny, do you care to explain?"

Johnny dropped his head and mumbled something Mac couldn't understand.

"I'm sorry. What was that?"

The boy lifted his gaze to Mac's, his lower lip protruding. "Amy and I found some baby rabbits out back."

"You shouldn't have taken them from their nest. They need their mother." Mac walked to the children and knelt next to them to peek into the box at two tiny balls of grayish brown fluff.

"We've been watching them for the past few days. I think their mother abandoned them." Johnny hovered over the box as though he was going to protect them.

"You don't know that for sure."

"Yes, Daddy. We saved them just like Colt. They're hungry."

"That's why I got them a bowl of milk, but I can't get them to drink."

Mac sighed heavily, tunneling his hand through his hair then rubbing the back of his neck, his muscles taut beneath his fingers. He wasn't sure what to say or do. He noticed that one rabbit's eyes weren't open yet as they squirmed together, nudging each other for comfort.

"Can we keep them, Daddy?"

"Oh, pumpkin, I don't know if that's what's best for them. We can't have animals like Colt does."

"Why not, Daddy?"

Mac stared into her big, brown eyes and couldn't come up with a reason she would accept. *Because I said so* wasn't going to work with her or Johnny. "We'll discuss this when I get home. I'm due at the hospital. I'll call Colt and talk to him about this on the way."

"What should we do about them being hungry?"

Johnny looked at Mac as though he would have the answer. What to do? He scratched his head and tried to think of a way to feed the babies something until he could find out what to do with them. When his daughter stared at him, too, her thumb still in her mouth, he retrieved his cell phone from his pocket and punched in Colt's number. He had to leave a message for the man to call him back. When he slipped his phone into his pocket, he faced the two children who were waiting for a solution to the babies' problem.

"I'll get an eyedropper and you can try to use it to feed the rabbits some milk. But don't do anything else until I return. Maybe

Colt will call me back by then. After you feed them, put the babies in the box and leave them alone. Is that understood?" Mac looked from Amy, who nodded, to Johnny, whose pout deepened into a scowl. "Johnny?"

"Yes," the ten-year-old muttered, clearly not happy with the order.

"Are you gonna see Aunt Casey?"

"I think she's working today. But I'm going up to see the children on the floor."

"How about Tess? Is she working?"

Mac was surprised by Johnny's questions. "I don't know. I'm not sure about her work schedule," he said, hating to admit the woman was avoiding him. "Have you talked to her lately?"

"She called yesterday to see how I was doing. She said something about taking me out for some ice cream."

"She did?"

"Yes, and me, too, Daddy. I like ice cream."

"Does she call you often?"

"Usually every day."

How is she? The question was on the tip of Mac's tongue, but he bit it back. He hadn't seen her in several weeks and was determined to change that fact. "You know I like ice cream, too." Now why in the

158

world had he said that?

"Then you can go with us." Amy peered at Johnny. "Right? Just like a family."

The hard edge in the boy's gaze softened as he looked at Amy and nodded. "We'll need to ask Tess first."

"Oh, she won't care. She's a nice lady."

Mac hoped Tess didn't care, because he was going to use the opportunity the children offered to be with her. He'd never seen anyone run as fast as she was from relationships and people. She was hurting inside, and he was determined to help her. The Lord had given him many blessings, and it was his duty to be there for others in need. And if he kept telling himself that was the only reason he wanted to see Tess, he might just come to believe it.

The children were all gathered around the table in the playroom, their faces eager. The nursing techs had managed to squeeze in two hospital beds with a boy and a girl who were bedridden. Quiet reigned where only a moment before laughter had filled the air when Tess had botched a magic trick. The deck of cards lay scattered all over the floor.

Tess allowed her gaze to peruse the colorfully decorated room before it settled on a little girl near her. "Kelly, you can be my assistant for this next feat of magic." From inside her oversize coat she pulled out a flattened top hat and popped it open, the sound punctuating the silence. "I want you to hold onto this hat as tight as you can." Nodding, the child took it. "Now, I'm going to pour this glass of water into the hat where it will disappear into thin air," Tess said with dramatic flair.

After emptying the glass, Tess took her wand, tapping the sides of the hat while the little girl held it above her. "Abracadabra and all that mumble jumble." Tess swept her arm wide, her gaze pinning each child for a second. "Now, who would like to wear this beautiful hat?"

When no one volunteered, Tess scanned the faces of the children again, making the corners of her mouth turn down in a frown. "Okay. I admit my last trick didn't work, but this one will."

One child in a wheelchair giggled.

"You don't believe me. Well, I'll prove it." Tess grasped the hat high in the air and then plopped it down onto her head. Water cascaded down her face, dripping into her eyes and splashing onto her clothes and the floor.

The children burst out laughing.

Through the strands of wet red hair obstructing her view, Tess saw Mac lounging against the door into the playroom. She flipped the hair back and gave an exaggerated sigh. "Oh, my, what could have possibly gone wrong?" She held out her hand toward a nursing tech. "A towel, please."

The woman handed her a tiny swatch of cloth to dry her face and clothes. Tess mopped at the water then twisted and twisted the cloth to wring it out, managing to squeeze out a few drops of liquid. While she sidestepped toward the door, her shoes made a funny squeaky noise that drew more laughter from the children. As she escaped down the hall, trying to run in her oversize shoes, she felt Mac's gaze on her as well as several of the children's. She came to a screeching halt at the door into the employee locker room, turned toward the playroom and tipped her top hat before disappearing inside.

She leaned against the door and let out a rush of air, the pounding of her heart having nothing to do with her swift getaway. Quickly she began removing her wet clown clothes, then her white streaked makeup, trying her best not to think about the man in the playroom. But all she could picture was his smiling face. All she could hear was his deep, rich laughter complementing the children's. And she could swear she had smelled sandalwood as she'd raced by him. Avoiding him certainly hadn't managed to diminish his effect on her.

So what was she going to do about it?

She didn't have an answer for that question. She wanted to be involved with Johnny, and the child was living with Mac. She was going to have to bite the bullet and put up with the man if she wanted to see Johnny. It wouldn't be easy, but surely she could be around Mac and his family and not have visions of having a family herself.

With her determination firmly in place, Tess marched down the hall toward the playroom and the sounds of children's voices excitedly talking. When she peeked into the room, intending to check out what was going on before heading to the cafeteria to grab something to eat, she saw Mac signing his name on anything and everything that was thrust at him. One little girl insisted he write "Mack Truck" on her bare arm, and her peals of laughter drowned out all the other children's voices.

"That tickled. Do this one, too. Please." The little girl smiled at Mac.

Mac took her other arm and made a big production out of it. All the other children quieted and watched. When Mac finished with a flourish, he scanned the faces of the boys and girls, his gaze finally coming to rest on Tess in the doorway. One corner of his mouth lifted in a lopsided grin while the room erupted in giggles and talking. Tess responded to the mischief twinkling in his eyes, returning his grin.

A boy in a wheelchair tapped Mac's arm, pulling his attention away. The child pointed to the cast on his leg, and Mac immediately signed it. Tess took the opportunity to move away from the playroom. If she walked fast, she could be at the elevator and on her way to the cafeteria before Mac realized she was gone. She punched the button and waited, glancing back several times as though any second he would appear and she would be dazzled with his presence, unable to escape. She made it safely onto the elevator, rode to the ground floor and hurried to the cafeteria, finally breathing a sigh of relief.

While she inspected the array of salads before her, she sensed someone come up behind her. The faint scent of sandalwood drifted to her seconds before Mac whispered close to her ear, "Did you think I'd let you get away that easily?"

Tess peered over her shoulder, smiled and said, "Whatever do you mean?"

"I saw you hurrying to the elevator. I thought I would let you think you'd escaped my clutches. But alas, Casey told me where you were going."

"I knew I was going to regret your sister working on my floor."

Tess grabbed the salad nearest her and slid her tray down the counter toward the hot entrees. When she glanced at what she had put on her tray, she frowned. Macaroni salad wasn't one of her favorites. As she told her order to the server, she noticed Mac pick up a tray, select a salad and move down the counter toward her.

Tess took piping hot roast beef, mashed potatoes and broccoli from the lady. She wondered if she could attribute the perspiration on her upper lip to the steam floating from the serving line. The server eyed Mac and heaped an extra large portion of roast beef and mashed potatoes on his plate, then drenched them in brown gravy.

"I guess she thinks you're a growing boy," Tess said as she pushed her tray toward the checkout person.

"Do I detect a note of envy in your voice?"

Tess stared at the food piled on his plate, watching him add a large slice of pecan pie to his tray. "I think I'm gaining weight just looking at your meal."

"Just so the nurse in you doesn't get too worked up over this high-calorie meal, I exercise every day. I usually don't eat this much."

"I'm worried about you." Tess handed the lady at the cash register the money for her lunch.

"Why?"

"You came to a hospital to overindulge in food? Hospital cafeterias aren't known for their culinary treats."

Mac followed her to a table in the corner near a large ficus tree. "True. But Casey told me this one has good food." He slipped into the chair next to her. "My sister is a fountain of information when it comes to this hospital. And now Amy has decided she wants to be a nurse. She's been practicing on her dolls. Her bedroom has been turned into a hospital."

"You have a beautiful daughter." Tess heard the wistful tone in her voice and hoped Mac didn't. She didn't want to get into a discussion of children and families.

"That she is. She's my life." Mac stared at his plate of food, the hand that held the fork poised in midair as though he were caught in a moment of reflection.

Tess clenched her teeth together to keep from asking questions about his deceased wife. It wasn't her place to delve into his past, and yet she wanted to know everything about him. She cleared her throat and asked, "How's Johnny doing?"

"I think he's settling in."

"Has Mrs. Hocks had any luck finding a relative?"

"No."

Tess took a bite of roast beef. "What if she doesn't?"

"I want to adopt Johnny."

Her gaze was riveted to Mac's. The noise level in the cafeteria was high, but suddenly everything seemed to fade away — all sounds, all the people. She saw and heard only Mac. "Have you said anything about this to him?"

Mac shook his head. "And I won't until Mrs. Hocks has exhausted all her leads and Johnny feels at home with us. I'm hoping that won't be too much longer. You should have seen Amy and him today. They found some baby rabbits and decided to take in strays like Colt."

"What did you do?"

"On the way over here Colt returned my call. We discussed what we should do. The kids are sure the mother rabbit was killed. Colt told me they might survive if I can get them to eat. Before I left, Johnny fed them some milk with an eyedropper. The rabbits were sleeping when I left."

"How small are they?"

"They can't be more than a week or two old. One of them has his eyes open. The other doesn't. I could hold one in my palm."

For a few seconds Tess stared at his hand and remembered his gentle touch. Her stomach flip-flopped. "Then you're going to keep the rabbits?"

"I have a hard time resisting those two kids. Besides, I'm a sucker for strays, too."

"For animals in trouble?"

"People, too."

The intensity of his regard robbed her of her next breath. She swallowed several times, the tightness in her throat threatening to snatch her voice. She knew in that moment she didn't want to be one of his charity cases. She wanted more, and that frightened her. She looked away and concentrated on cutting her roast beef into bite size pieces, aware of his gaze on her. Her hands quivered.

"When I took my first psychology class in college, I became hooked on trying to figure out what makes people do the things they do." Mac sipped his coffee, peering at her over the rim of his cup.

"Some people don't like to be analyzed."

"Some people need someone to help them through their problems. They're too close to them. They can't get a good perspective of them."

"Is that what you do at the halfway house?" Tess asked, hoping to steer the conversation away from her.

"I told you I'm a good listener. That's what I mostly do. That and get people to understand why they're doing what they do."

"Stray people aren't like stray animals."

"But both need understanding and love."

When he said the word *love*, for a moment she allowed herself to wonder what it would be like loved by a man like Mac. Then she remembered the pain such intense emotions caused and pushed the dream away. "How are the puppies? Is Johnny taking care of his?"

Mac didn't answer her right away. He chewed his food slowly, his eyes narrowed on her face as though he were contemplating not letting her get away with changing the subject of their conversation. Finally he said, "Yes. I've been impressed with how well. Frisky sleeps in his room in a box. Sometimes I've found the puppy sleeping with Johnny when I check on him before going to bed. They're usually inseparable. That's why I should have known something was up when both Amy and Johnny put their puppies in the utility room this morning."

"It looks like your trip to Colt's farm may have triggered something."

"Yeah, I'm gonna have a house full of stray animals if I don't put my foot down." Mac cut into his pecan pie.

Tess watched him bring the bite to his mouth. Hers watered. "Wait till Casey hears about the rabbits. Your sister will encourage them."

"Yeah, that's what I'm afraid of. Amy's gonna be staying with Mom and Casey this weekend while I'm camping with Johnny and some of the kids from church."

"Chaperoning? You are a brave man."

"And I need a chaperone for the girls. Justin and his wife are coming, but Mary could use another woman to help her. Care to come along?"

"Me?"

"Yes. You could spend time with Johnny. He talks about you all the time."

"He does?"

"Come on. What do you say? I know you aren't working."

"How? Oh, never mind. Casey." The idea he was asking his sister about her made her

169

blush. "Let me think about it."

"There'll be twelve children, seven boys and five girls, going, ranging in ages from ten to fourteen. Johnny doesn't say anything, but I think he's excited. I talked with his doctor, and he gave me the okay. Johnny's recovering quite well."

"Yeah, I know."

"Now all we have to do is work on his spirit. He's really taken to going to church with us, and this youth group has been wonderful for him."

Was that why she felt such a kinship with Johnny? They were both wounded in spirit. Tess knew she didn't want to pass up an opportunity to spend some time with the boy. She'd missed him these past few weeks. Talking to him on the phone wasn't the same thing as seeing him, making sure with her own two eyes that he was doing all right. Maybe it was time for her to stop trying to avoid Mac and let things happen naturally. Maybe it was time to face her fear of getting close to another man. Her life right now was certainly less than fulfilling.

"How did you convince Johnny to leave Frisky behind?"

"It wasn't easy, but Casey promised to take special care of her, and of course, Amy did, too."

"Will I have to hike much?"

"You probably do more walking on the pediatric floor than you'll do this weekend. Does this mean you'll go?"

Tess inhaled a deep breath and nodded. The smile that touched Mac's mouth sent her heart slamming against her chest.

"I just knew you wouldn't let — Johnny down."

A finely honed tension held Tess immobile. She felt as though she had plunged over a cliff without a lifeline. She was doing this for Johnny, she told herself and knew that was a lie. She was doing it for herself. She wanted to get to know Peter MacPherson, and it was time she did.

Chapter Nine

Tess really wished she had asked where they were going to camp. In the middle of a mountain range wasn't her idea of a most ideal place to spend her weekend. But then she should have realized they would probably camp in the Rockies, since Denver sat at the foot of them. When she was around Mac, she sometimes forgot to think straight.

Adjusting her backpack, she followed Mac along the trail that would take them to their campsite. The excited voices of the children penetrated the morning silence. The scent of pine and earth saturated the air with a soothing aroma that seeped into Tess and eased her distress. The crystal-blue sky with not a cloud in sight promised the day would be a beautiful one. She listened to the snap of twigs and leaves beneath her boots and to the laughter of one of the girls ahead of her and felt content for the moment. She had always loved the mountains. Maybe she could put her memories behind her and enjoy the weekend for what it was — a time to get to know Mac and Johnny better.

Johnny's warm greeting when she'd climbed into Mac's car had given her hope. Mac was doing something right because she had never seen the child so happy, relaxed. His skin looked healthy, and his eyes were bright. Mac was a good father and deserved a household full of children. If Mac adopted Johnny, how would that affect her?

"Look, a hummingbird," one of the girls said, pointing toward a tree.

Tess paused to watch the tiny bird move its wings so fast it was hard to see them. It hovered for a few seconds then darted off. As she turned her gaze toward the trail, out of the trees came a deer, soaring across the path and bounding into the thick brush on the other side.

Not a word was spoken for a full minute as though everyone was waiting for another deer to cross, then all of a sudden every child began to talk and gesture toward where the deer had disappeared into the forest. A cool breeze stirred Tess's hair as she marveled at the grace of the animal and the beauty about her. She loved the outdoors and used to call it God's playground.

"I hope we see a bear," one of the older children said at the front of the line.

"I want to see a wolf."

"How about a mountain lion," Johnny added to the list.

Tess thought of those animals, and her eyes grew round. "Mac, are you prepared if we do?"

"Chances are we won't. Don't worry. Probably the biggest animal we'll see is that deer."

"I hope you're right. While all three of those animals are beautiful to look at, I prefer steel bars or glass between me and them. I know my limitations and how fast I can run."

"Running away from your problems isn't the best solution. They'll only follow you and take you over," he whispered to her. Then in a louder voice he said, "Let's keep moving. We have a ways to go to the campsite."

Mac's advice stayed with Tess the rest of the trip to the campsite. For the past two years she had been running away from what had happened in South America. She had tried to deal with it, but each time had felt overwhelmed with guilt and emotion until she had shoved it back in the dark recesses of her mind to examine later. Was later finally here? She asked herself that as she flung her backpack to the ground and scanned their home for the weekend, nestled under a canopy of pines and aspens.

Johnny came up next to her and shrugged off his backpack, too. "I've never been camping. Are there really bears and mountain lions around?"

"Nothing for you to worry about."

He puffed out his chest. "I ain't worried for myself. I don't want anything to happen to the — girls. All that screaming wouldn't be pleasant to the ears."

"I suppose you're right. Mac tells me I shouldn't worry."

"If one comes around, I'll protect ya."

She smiled at the boy. "Thanks." She noticed the pale cast to his cheeks and added, "I need to rest. Will you keep me company?"

He looked at the others sitting and said, "Sure. Then I'll need to help with my tent. Mac said something about finding firewood, too."

"If you help me put up my tent, I'll help you, then we both can look for wood."

"A deal." Johnny grinned, easing onto the ground with his legs crossed Indian-style. "Have you put up a tent before?"

"Yes," she answered, recalling other times she'd camped in the mountains a continent away.

"Is it hard?"

"A piece of cake."

An hour later Tess wished she had looked at the directions before declaring to Johnny how easy it was to assemble a tent. His was one of the big ones that would hold four boys. Finally Mac came to their rescue, taking the center pole that held the tent up and driving it into the ground.

"Okay, so I had the wrong pole. Anyone could make that mistake," Tess said while Mac continued to issue directions to Johnny, who scrambled to obey them.

The tent was erected in less than five minutes. Tess stood by and watched the whole process. Johnny gave Mac a high five before making his way to her, pride in his step.

"The one I used in the past was entirely different," Tess said in her defense, pleased at how well Johnny was bonding with Mac. The boy needed a man in his life, and Mac was perfect for the job.

"Mac told me your tent is simpler, and I should be able to do it by myself."

In other words, stand back while I show you what I've learned. Tess was only too happy to let Johnny put the tent up by himself. She had learned quickly that the child had had few positive strokes in his life and responded to them when given appropriately.

While Johnny proceeded to work on her tent, Tess spied Mac talking to a child who had scraped his knee. Seeing him soothe the child, who was crying, she began to envision him with a horde of his own children surrounding him, her next to him. The picture nearly knocked the breath from her as she quickly looked away. Okay, he would make a good father — was in fact already a good father — but that didn't mean she had to be the mother. She needed to rid her mind of those thoughts, and quickly, before she did something risky — like fall in love with Mac.

Tess stared at the tent she was to share with Mary and couldn't bring herself to walk to it. A cool breeze blew down from the mountaintop, ruffling her hair and reminding her of other times. She shivered and pulled her light jacket close, folding her arms across her chest to ward off the chill burrowing deep into her bones that had nothing to do with the temperature.

All day she had kept herself busy with the children and hadn't had time to reflect. Now she couldn't ignore the thin mountain air, the feeling she was on top of the world looking down on life. She couldn't ignore the memories.

Tess looked around the campsite at the five tents set up in a circle with a large fire in the center. Not long before, the children had roasted marshmallows over that fire and Mac had told them Bible stories of Christ's journey to save humankind. There had been times Kevin and Tess had sat outside at night, listening to nature, breathing the fresh, clean air and discussing the Lord and their mission in South America.

What had gone wrong? What had she done wrong? Those questions taunted her, nibbling at her fragile composure. She shuddered, trying desperately to stop the flood of memories. This wasn't the time to remember.

"Cold?" Mac asked, sitting next to her on a log in front of the fire.

"A little."

"Here, let's move the log closer to the fire."

He stood and repositioned the piece of wood. Now if Tess wanted to, she could reach out and warm her hands over the flames. After zipping her jacket, she did just that and noticed their slight tremor.

"Better?"

"Yes. I forgot how cold it can get once the sun goes down even though it's the middle of May."

"Up on the top of this mountain there's still snow. You go high enough, you can leave summer behind in July."

Yes, it had been that way in the Andes, too, Tess remembered, and wished again she could forget that part of her life.

"But your sleeping bag will be warm," Mac added, poking the fire with a stick.

A few sparks spewed into the air, caught on the breeze and swirled. Tess watched them disappear in the darkness, wishing her problems could disappear, as well. "Thanks for loaning me one. I'm not equipped for camping."

"We do this several times a year with different groups of children. It's good for them to get away from the city and commune with nature, not to sit in front of the TV or play video games for hours. When I'm up here, I feel closer to God. He's always around us, but here His presence seems sharper and clearer to me."

Once she'd thought that very thing. Was that why she'd been sure the Lord would answer her prayer that day in the Andes? Tess looked again at the tent she was to sleep in. "I guess we should turn in. It's quieted down."

"Finally. I think the kids completely wore Mary and Justin out."

"Mary's pregnant. She tires easily."

"What's Justin's excuse for turning in early?"

"Sympathy exhaustion?"

Mac laughed. "Yeah, I could see my little brother doing that."

"You have a wonderful family. You're very close."

"There isn't anything I wouldn't do for them. My parents instilled in us how important a sense of family is."

"You're lucky to have such a large, warm family. I was an only child and always wanted brothers and sisters. I swore when I got married I wouldn't have just one child."

Mac tossed the stick into the fire and watched the flames lick at the wood for a few seconds before dying back. "There's nothing wrong with having just one child. There are advantages to being an only child."

"What?" Tess asked, remembering the times she'd played by herself because there was no one else around.

"You don't have to share as much."

"Peter MacPherson, I doubt very seriously you want Amy to grow up not knowing how to share. I've seen you with her."

He threw her a sheepish look. "Okay, you're right. But I'm happy with having just Amy — and Johnny, if it's the Lord's plan for me to adopt him."

"You're a young man. You could have more children." The second she'd spoken, she wanted to bite her tongue. "I mean you don't know what the future will hold for you."

"Some things I do have control over." A hard edge entered his voice.

"No one has control totally over their future. I've seen you with the children today. You're a wonderful father. You have a lot to teach them."

"I can be around children as I am now and have an influence over them without being their father."

"Amy should have brothers and sisters. Take it from an only child."

Mac didn't say anything, the tight set of his jaw attesting to some inner struggle.

"Look how Amy has taken to Johnny. He tells me she follows him around."

"Does that bother him?"

"Are you kidding? He's never had a sibling and he's eating it up. She hangs on his every word."

"I know living with us has been an adjustment for him, but it's been good to have him at the house." Mac rose, extending his hand to help Tess up. "We have a full day tomorrow."

When his fingers closed around hers and

he pulled her up, she came within inches of him. His scent drove all others away, centering her thoughts and senses on the man before her. In the golden glow of the firelight she saw his gaze soften as it took in her features, finally coming to rest on her mouth. Her lips tingled under the intensity of his regard.

He grazed his fingertips across her lower lip. "I'm glad you decided to come this weekend."

She couldn't say the words, *I'm glad, too.* They were stuck in her tight throat. She couldn't take her gaze from his. His eyes in the firelight appeared as two pieces of molten silver, mesmerizing her.

He cupped her face and leaned down, his lips brushing hers like a warm gentle breeze. The muscles in her legs liquefied. She grasped his shoulders to keep from collapsing against him while he slanted his mouth against hers and claimed her in a deep, heart-wrenching kiss. She felt it from the top of her head to the tip of her toes, like an electrical current that zipped through her body.

Nearby she heard an owl hoot, startling her. Gasping, she jumped back, her hand coming up to cover her mouth.

"I'm not sorry I kissed you. I've wanted to

do that for a long time, Tess."

And she wasn't sorry he had kissed her. She wasn't even surprised by her intense reaction to his kiss. She'd anticipated it from the first time she'd laid eyes on him in the waiting room.

When she didn't say anything, he covered the distance that separated them and caressed a wayward strand of hair from her cheek. "Are you all right?"

The tenderness in his expression dissolved all rational thought. All she could do was stare into his eyes and want to become lost in them.

"Tess?"

One corner of her mouth quirked. "Sorry. I'm fine. Really. I was so wrapped up in you — your kiss that the owl just surprised me. That's all."

"If you're sure?"

"Very. Now, I'd better get to bed or I'll be worthless tomorrow. I can bet the children will be up at the crack of dawn."

Tess took a shaky step back from Mac.

"I can guarantee it." He walked with her to the small tent she was sharing with Mary. "Good night."

Tess crawled inside, peering across the dying fire at Mac who stood in front of the tent he shared with his brother. She ran her fingertips across her lips and imagined the feel of his mouth on hers. Just thinking about it sent her pulse racing.

When she snuggled between the covers of her sleeping bag, she couldn't get the picture of Mac out of her mind. She closed her eyes but still saw him. She was afraid the man was going to haunt her dreams. Burrowing into the warmth surrounding her, she forced her thoughts away from Peter MacPherson for all of ten seconds. As exhaustion unfolded and spread through her, she felt herself sink into a world full of hopes. . . .

The harsh glare of lights and the heat radiating from them made rivulets of perspiration roll down Tess's face. She wiped her hand across her forehead and tried to smile at the audience. The corners of her mouth quivered from the strain.

"Now, Miss Morgan, the million-dollar question is —" the emcee paused for a few seconds, shuffling the index cards in his hands before selecting one and reading "— why were you allowed to live while everyone else was killed? You have one minute to come up with an answer."

The loud ticking of the clock started counting down her seconds.

Frantically Tess searched her thoughts for a

reason, but all she could focus on was the ticktock of the clock reverberating through her mind. Why? Why me?

The buzzer blared. The audience quieted, waiting to hear her reply. She scanned their faces, desperately wishing the answer was written on them. Their features dissolved into blank masks.

"I don't know," she finally said to the emcee.

He thrust his face into hers and shouted, "Why don't you know? Why were you saved and not the others?"

The audience took up the chant. Why? Why?

"I don't know. I don't know."

Tess bolted up in her sleeping bag, breathing shallow gasps of air, sweat pouring off her as though she had been standing under the glare of harsh lights. Her heartbeat thundered in her ears. Distraught, she looked around, trying to figure out where she was. Reality crept in. Tess stared at Mary sleeping next to her, the soft sound of her breathing suddenly reminding her of the ticktock of the clock in her dream.

Tess dropped her head, burying her face in her shaking hands while drawing in deep breaths to calm herself. She felt as if the tent walls enclosed her in a trap. Shoving back the sleeping bag, she grabbed a blanket and scrambled outside, not wanting to awaken Mary.

She inhaled deep, cleansing breaths, saturated with the scent of the mountain. Her heartbeat slowed to a decent pace as she walked to the log and sat. She wrapped the blanket around her, then rested her elbows on her knees, her chin cupped in her hands. In the moonlight that filtered through the trees she stared at the black pit where the fire had been and tried to find some kind of peace. It eluded her as though she tried to hold a snowflake in her palm.

"Can't sleep, either?"

She had been so deep in thought she hadn't heard Mac approach until he sat down beside her on the log, clicking off the flashlight he carried. Blackness surrounded them, giving the fantasy that they were alone in the middle of nowhere.

"Bad dream," she answered before she realized what she'd said.

"Want to tell me about it?" He lit a lantern, throwing a circle of light about them and shattering the illusion of isolation.

No — yes. She slanted a look at his profile, his gaze trained straight ahead. The glow from the lantern softened his features, coaxing her to tell him about the nightmare — about South America and Kevin. "For the past two years I've been running away and I've just come to the conclusion you can't, not from yourself. You're right. There's a time when everything catches up with you."

"Tell me about the dream."

"I'm a game show contestant and the emcee asks me the final question and I can't answer it."

"What's the question?"

The gentleness in his voice soothed her. She could do this. She looked sideways at him. "Why were you allowed to live while everyone else was killed?"

The question hung in the air between them for a few seconds. Then she heard Mac suck in a sharp breath, his gaze zeroing in on hers. "What happened, Tess?"

"I was a nurse at a mission in the Andes. My fiancé and I had decided to serve two years overseas before we married and started a family. Kevin had just finished his residency in family practice. We had been there for a year when a band of guerrillas came into the village. They killed everyone but me. They left me for dead, but I survived the gunshot wound." Her voice caught. She swallowed hard and continued in a tone that mirrored the trembling in her body. "I watched Kevin die, and there was nothing I could do to help him or anyone else in the village. The only way I made it was by pretending I was dead, too. Thankfully they didn't check."

Mac grasped her hand in his, the warmth of his touch a balm to her tattered nerves. "I'm so sorry, Tess. No one should have to go through something like that."

His comforting words reached out and caressed the pain in her heart. "When they left, I tried to help Kevin. I was too late. He died in my arms. After that, I passed out. The next thing I remember is waking up in a hospital bed in the capital."

His grip tightened. "Is that why you've turned away from God?"

She twisted, staring at him through glistening eyes. "Don't you understand? Kevin was a good man. A good Christian who only wanted to serve the Lord and help people through his medicine. He had so much to give in the name of the Lord. More than me. Why did he die and I live?" One tear slipped down her cheek and fell onto their clasped hands.

"Sometimes God has plans for people that aren't what we think they should be. We have to have faith He knows what is best in the long run. Kevin is with God now. The Lord has something else in mind for you."

Tess squeezed her eyes closed for a long moment, wanting to shut the world out. "When I went to his funeral, his mother couldn't understand why I was alive and her son was dead. She fell apart in church. I barely managed to get through the service." Recalling that awful scene, she shuddered.

"You have much to give to others."

"But I don't save lives like Kevin did."

"There are ways to save a person that have nothing to do with medicine. Look how you took Johnny under your wing. If it hadn't been for you, Johnny wouldn't be living with Amy and me right now. The Lord hasn't given up on you. Don't give up on Him."

Still Tess could remember begging God to save Kevin or to take her instead. The memory haunted her. "I wish it were that simple."

"But it is."

The one thing that had nagged at her came to the foreground. "Kevin was a better Christian than me. He was much more devoted than me. So why did God take him and not me?"

"It's okay that you survived. You don't need to feel guilty."

"I wish I could believe that."

"You need to take a good hard look at the

people you influence. Besides Johnny, Amy adores you, and I care about you very much. Then how about all the children you entertain with your clown therapy or help while they're in the hospital."

She pulled her hands from his grasp and rose, restless, as though her nerves were stretched beyond their limit and would break any second. "I might as well tell you everything." She let out a long breath. "Kevin was in the village that day because I talked him out of going to the capital until the following day. I thought it was going to rain and I didn't want us to get stuck traveling on the trail in a downpour." She whirled to face Mac. "He would be alive today if it wasn't for me."

Mac flinched as though she had hit him. In the dim light she could see his features pale. Now he knew the full extent of her responsibility in Kevin's death.

"So you see, Mac, there isn't much you can say to make me feel any less guilty. A good man died because of me."

Mac shot to his feet and gripped her upper arms. "Don't say that. *You* had nothing to do with it. You didn't pull the trigger. You can't foresee the future. You made a judgment call on the facts as you knew them. You are not to blame for his death."

She wrenched herself free, stepping away from him. "I saw how you looked at me when I told you."

"You saw my anguish over my wife's death in my face. Your words were so similar to what I felt right after Sheila died."

"What do you mean? Your wife died in childbirth."

"She didn't want to have a family. I'm the one who wanted to start having children and talked her into it. She would be alive today if I hadn't. So you see, you aren't the only one with guilt over another's death."

"Is that why you don't want any more children?"

"Isn't that enough?"

"Dying in childbirth isn't common."

"I won't be responsible for putting another woman in danger if I have anything to do with it. I can't risk that kind of loss ever again."

His confession stunned her. Words failed her. She clenched then flexed her hands. Slowly she curled her fingers into fists, her nails digging into her palms. So much pain. So much guilt — on both their parts. How would they begin to heal? To forgive themselves? Tess wondered.

"When Sheila died, I don't know what I

would have done if it weren't for my faith in the Lord. The first time I held Amy I felt so lost. God gave me the strength to live each day. He can do the same for you, Tess."

She wanted to believe Mac, but she could remember her pleas that went unanswered in that mountain village. "What happened to me isn't the same as what happened to you."

"You're right. I had the support and love of my family to help me. I had a little baby girl to take care of. I imagine you were all alone to deal with your grief. What I'm trying to tell you now is that you aren't really alone. God is with us always. Let go of your guilt and embrace our Father."

She spun away, turning her back to him, hunching her shoulders as she drew in on herself. "I wish I could."

He laid his hand on her. "Let me help you. Come with my family to church again. Open your heart to the possibilities of the Lord."

Placing her palm over her heart, she felt its steady beat, evidence she'd survived that day in the mountains. She knew she had to do something to change the direction of her life. She loved nursing and dressing up as a clown to entertain sick children, but she was discovering that she needed something more. It was as though she had put her life back together after South America, but there were missing pieces to the jigsaw puzzle that left gaping holes in the overall picture.

"Both Amy and Johnny would love to have you accompany us."

Just Amy and Johnny? She wanted to ask, but bit her bottom lip to keep from saying what she really wanted to.

"Amy's still talking about our trip out to Colt's. And she wanted me to tell you again she was sorry about what Buttons did."

"Next time I know not to ask to hold the puppy."

His chuckles, close to her ear, whispered against her neck. "I never saw someone move so fast in the front seat of my car."

Tess faced Mac. "It's not every day I have the privilege of an animal using me like a piece of newspaper."

"She was just overexcited to see you."

"That kind of excitement I can do without. But tell Amy again for me that it wasn't her fault."

"Come to dinner next week and tell her yourself. I know they would love to show you the rabbits and how much the puppies have grown."

"Okay," she said, aware she was committing herself to more than dinner. She was risking her heart again. She knew she couldn't resist the lure of Mac and his family.

Chapter Ten

Tess checked the address again, making sure she was on the right street. The houses needed fresh paint. One had a broken window patched with boards. Another had foot-tall weeds growing in its small front yard, which was littered with rusted car parts.

Tess spied Mac standing on the porch of a large two-story house on the corner. Painted recently, the halfway house had a new roof. The lawn was mowed, and the hedge in front was trimmed neatly. She slowed to a stop at the curb, craning her neck to stare at the shingled roof from which Mac had fallen and broken his leg. She shuddered at the long fall and thought how lucky he was that his leg was the only thing he'd broken that day. She climbed from her car, locked it then headed up the sidewalk. Mac descended the steps and met her at the bottom.

"I wish you'd let me pick you up. This neighborhood isn't the best." Mac casually placed his hand at the small of her back.

"After what I've seen and lived through, this place is a piece of cake."

He grimaced. "That still doesn't mean I can't be concerned for your safety."

"I could say the same thing to you."

"Ah, a feminist."

She stopped at the front door and looked deep into his eyes. "No, a bullet will tear through your flesh as easily as mine. It doesn't know if you're male or female."

"Then I guess we will worry about each other."

"That's what friends do."

"Yes, friends," he murmured and pulled the door open to allow her to enter.

"I'm not surprised at the location of the halfway house. Have any of your neighbors complained?"

"A few. But there have been no problems in the two years we have been here, and the complaints have died down."

Some of the tension siphoned from Tess at that news. Part of the reason she'd decided to volunteer at the halfway house was that she wanted to see for herself what Mac did that was so important to him. The other reason was to check out the place. She could no longer deny that Mac was special to her. She needed to assess how safe he was. He

196

came here almost every day. She cared about him and didn't want to lose him — as a friend, she added quickly, the hollowness of the declaration ringing through her mind.

"I think our good neighbors have learned to ignore us, and that makes it easier. One less problem to deal with." Mac motioned toward the living area. "Let me give you a quick tour."

Tess scanned the room. There were two comfortable, worn-looking couches and three overstuffed easy chairs, all surrounding a television set. Several end tables held lamps and coasters, and one had a stack of magazines. In the center of the coffee table, in front of one of the navy blue sofas, was a large Bible. Near the picture window that faced the street was a schefflera, a good six feet tall. One man sat in a chair watching CNN and chewing gum while another had propped his feet on the scarred coffee table with his head resting on the cushion, his eyes closed.

"Fred, anything happening in the world?" Mac asked the man in the chair.

"Nope. Not a thing," Fred answered between smacks of his gum.

"Well, I guess that's a good thing."

"No news is good news." The man

cracked a smile, revealing one of his front teeth was missing.

"Is Harry asleep?"

"Guess so. He hasn't stirred since I've been here."

Mac frowned but didn't say anything. He signaled for Tess to follow him into the dining room, then the kitchen.

Once the door shut behind her, Tess asked, "Is everything all right with Harry?"

"He's new to the house. Came at the end of last week. I haven't been able to reach him like the others, but with the Lord's help I will." Mac passed through the kitchen, saying hello to Tom, the cook this week, and headed for the office in the back. "I counsel in here if the group is a small one or there's only one person. Sometimes we have large groups and we meet in the game room, through there." He pointed to a door leading from the office. "That's where you'll see anyone who has a medical problem. If you think they need to see a doctor, let me know. I can arrange that."

"How many men are living here?"

"Fifteen. We're almost to capacity."

"Do they stay long?"

"Not too long. This is a transition place for them. With luck by the time they leave here they have a job and have been off drugs or alcohol for a while."

Tess inspected the large office with a desk in one corner and a grouping of chairs in front of book-filled shelves at the other end. This was where Mac spent a lot of his time. The room reflected his character, from a Bible on the desk to a casual lived-in look that gave off no pretensions. "Are you the only counselor?"

"No, there are three of us who work here part-time."

"Do they all volunteer their time like you do?"

He looked uncomfortable. "Yes. The network of volunteers has grown since I've gotten to know some people at your hospital."

She noticed over the weeks she'd become better acquainted with Mac that he rarely wanted to talk about the good things he did for others. That was another part of his character she liked. He quietly went through life trying to right wrongs in the name of the Lord.

"Ready to get started?"

With a nod she walked toward the door Mac had indicated. "After I see everyone, what else would you like me to do?"

Mac smiled. "I imagine that will take most of the afternoon."

Tess had her doubts, since there weren't that many people in the house at the moment. Except for the television the place was quiet. She didn't hear any footsteps from the floor above. But according to Mac, they had a nurse conduct a clinic once a week, so he must know what he was talking about.

Several hours later Tess realized it wasn't just the men in the house who came to the clinic, but people who lived in the neighborhood. She saw several women and children with symptoms ranging from a cough to what she suspected was a broken arm. She set up that woman with an appointment to get her arm x-rayed immediately.

Mac stuck his head in the doorway and asked, "How's it going?"

"So this place serves as a free clinic to the area?"

"That's one of the reasons the neighbors don't complain much any more. Some of these people never get any medical attention except what we have here. Once a month a doctor comes to the clinic. Otherwise it's a nurse. They don't much care. It's more than they had before we set up shop."

"Your foundation funds all this?"

"This is one of my projects."

Tess saw Tom standing in the entrance

with his head bowed. "Can I help you?"

The man looked up hesitantly. "I burned my hand a few days ago. I just wanted you to check it."

"Sure." Tess sent Tom a reassuring smile, hoping to ease some of his shyness.

Slowly he shuffled across the game room and sat in the chair in front of Tess. She waited for him to show her his hand. Hesitantly Tom raised his arm, his eyes downcast. She unwrapped the food-stained bandage, revealing a red and ugly-looking second-degree burn.

"This must have hurt bad."

"Still does, ma'am."

"Well, let me see what I can do to help you."

"I sure would appreciate anything you can do. I can't hold no knife in this hand, and I ain't too good with my left hand."

"Knife?"

"To cut up the vegetables for dinner, ma'am."

"Of course." Tess felt Mac's gaze on her as she worked to clean the burn and wrap it in a fresh bandage. She tingled from the touch of his eyes.

When she was through with Tom and he had left, she rose and stretched her cramped muscles, aware that Mac was still in the doorway to his office watching her. "I've enjoyed this. I don't know if I can volunteer every week because of my schedule at the hospital, but I would like to help out more."

Mac crossed the room. "That would be great. This place depends on its volunteers. I hope one day to expand services to the neighborhood. I'd like to have a doctor here more often and nurses here more than once a week." He stopped next to her. "You're very good with the patients, young and old. I like watching you work."

His praise wiped all thoughts from her mind. She felt the color in her cheeks flare at the same time a pleased feeling encased her in warmth. He reached toward her.

Shouts erupted from the living room. Without a second's hesitation, Mac spun and raced toward the yelling. Tess hastened after him, the loud voices suddenly too quiet. When she entered, she stopped inside the doorway, her gaze riveted to Harry, who stood over Fred in the chair. Anger marred the lines of Harry's face. His hands were fisted at his sides, his body conveying such rage that he appeared brittle, ready to break in two.

Mac moved close to the pair. "Harry, can I help you? Is something wrong?" His voice was soft, even.

202

His jaw clamped shut, Harry swung his gaze to Mac, a few feet from him. "He turned the station."

Fred, whose features were pale, spoke. "I thought he was asleep. I was tired of the news."

Harry glared at Fred. "Well, I wasn't asleep and I was listening to the news. Turn it back."

"I don't want to." The stubborn set of his mouth attested to Fred's mounting bravery now that others were in the room.

Harry leaned down, placing both hands on the arms of the chair and caging the other man against the back. "Turn back to CNN."

He spat out each word slowly and with such fury that Tess stepped back. Her heart pounded against her chest. Her palms were sweaty. The air in the room churned with intense emotions as though someone had switched a blender on high.

Mac shifted forward. "Harry, I'm glad you're up. It's time for our counseling session. You can watch the news afterward." Mac pitched his voice low, a calming sound, meant to subdue.

"I don't wanna talk to you now. I want to watch the news." Harry bent closer to Fred, their faces only inches apart.

Tess held her breath when Mac laid his hand on Harry's shoulder. The man tried to shrug it off. When that didn't work, he spun and faced Mac, forgetting about Fred. Fred quickly squeezed out of his seat and scrambled out of the room while Harry glared at Mac for daring to interrupt him. The sound of Fred's fleeing footsteps on the stairs echoed in Tess's mind, competing with the thundering of her heartbeat in her ears.

"You'll be able to when we're through, Harry. You accepted counseling as a condition for living here."

Some of the tension dissolved in Tess at the continual calming sound of Mac's voice, as though this type of incident happened every day and wasn't any big deal. She hoped Harry responded in a similar fashion. She gauged the man's reaction to Mac's words and saw a slight relaxing of the firm line of his jaw. Harry's sharp gaze mellowed as he instinctively followed Mac's example of taking deep breaths. Tess found herself doing it, too, and more of her tension eased.

Mac patiently waited for Harry to bring himself under control. Sweat beaded the man's forehead and rolled down his face. He clenched and unclenched his hands, but finally, after a few minutes of silence, his shoulders sagged and he dropped his head.

"Come on, Harry, let's talk about this in my office," Mac said, moving toward the doorway. "I know things haven't been easy for you since you came."

Tess stepped to the side and allowed both men to leave. When the room was empty, she collapsed onto the couch, all the energy draining from her body. When she'd looked into Harry's eyes, she'd seen hate and such anger she'd been frightened he would do something harmful to Fred — or Mac.

Thankfully Mac had deflated the man's rage, but what would happen next time if he couldn't? That question scared her more than the encounter she had just witnessed.

She headed to the game room, determined to stay until Mac emerged from his office safely. She glanced out the window and noticed it was getting late. She had a million things she needed to do at home, as well as errands to run, but she couldn't leave. The sound of Harry's raised voice sent her across the room to hover near the door in case Mac needed her. She wasn't sure what she could do. Harry was almost as large as Mac, and she was sure Mac could take care of himself in a physical fight, but if anything happened to Mac — She wouldn't allow herself to finish that thought.

Thirty minutes later, Mac and Harry

came out of the office. Harry hurried up the stairs while Mac watched him. Then Mac turned toward her, and she saw the weariness in his features. The dullness in his eyes and the tired lines on his face underscored how emotionally drained he was after the tension-charged encounter.

Tess went to him, only wanting to comfort and offer words of encouragement. "You did a great job of defusing the situation."

"Just part of the job." He shrugged off the compliment.

"How often do you have to do that?"

She hoped the panic didn't sound in her voice, but Mac looked at her sharply for a long moment before answering, "Not often, thankfully, but some of these men have a lot of emotional baggage to deal with. Until they do they often won't succeed in overcoming their addiction." He peered at his watch. "Why are you still here? Didn't you tell me you had to leave by four-thirty?"

She blushed. "Would you believe I wanted to make sure nothing happened with Harry?"

"And what would you have done?"

"I'm not sure. I didn't think that far. Call 911? Rush in and stop him?"

Mac grinned. "Let's see, you're five feet

four inches and he's over six-two. How were you going to stop him? Jump on his back?"

"Okay. You can quit laughing. That man was very angry when you two disappeared into your office an hour ago. I wasn't about to leave you here alone."

"There are at least five other men here, Tess." The corners of his eyes crinkled. "But I like the idea you were going to save me. Not many women have said that to me."

"And I'm not going to make that mistake again."

He reached up and cupped his hand along her jawline. "You can protect me anytime you want." He stared long and hard into her eyes. "I need to leave soon. I'll walk you to your car."

"Are you trying to protect me now?"

"This isn't the safest neighborhood, especially as it gets darker."

Tess gathered her purse and the sweater she had brought. "As you know, I parked right out front."

"Are you still coming to the church festival on Saturday with us?"

"I'm looking forward to it. I miss seeing Amy and Johnny."

"They miss you."

"How are the rabbits doing?"

"Good. The kids agreed to take the rabbits to Colt's on Sunday."

"They're giving up on the idea of a shelter for stray animals?"

"Not exactly. They think the country is a better place for their rabbits than the city." He leaned around her to open her car door. "I won't be surprised if they find another stray animal soon."

The scent of sandalwood drifted to her, making her acutely aware of the man near her. "I think you're right."

"I just hope it's nothing too outlandish. I remember Casey finding a skunk once."

"Oh, that could be a problem." Tess slid behind the driver's seat.

"A smelly problem."

"Maybe you'd better stock tomato juice in the pantry just in case."

His laughter blended with the sounds of the neighborhood, a car starting down the street, someone mowing a small patch of grass. "Not a bad idea. We'll pick you up at three on Saturday. Be ready for some fun and relaxation."

With a nod, she turned her key in the ignition.

Mac stepped back and watched her drive away. Every time he was with her he felt another brick around his heart crumble. He'd started out with friendship in mind. He'd sensed her need for spiritual help. Now he knew he had been fooling himself. He was falling for her and he wasn't sure that was wise for either of them. She was afraid to risk her heart, and he realized after his marriage to Sheila that he could never settle for anything but total commitment from a woman. Tess wanted a large family, and he knew he wasn't prepared to give her that. Nope, it wasn't a good idea to get too emotionally involved with Tess. But was it too late? Mac wondered as he headed inside the halfway house.

"How many cups of coffee does that make for the day?" Delise said as she plopped down beside Tess at the kitchen table.

"Five, and before you say anything I know that isn't good. But it's that or I'm gonna fall asleep at the church festival. Better yet on the ride to the place."

"Yeah, what's been going on? For the past few nights I've heard you up and about at all hours."

"Bad dream." A chill shimmered down Tess's length when she thought about the nightmare she'd had after the incident at the halfway house. She shook her head as though that would rid her mind of the image of Mac dying in his office with Harry standing over him. She could still hear her screams.

"Well, it must be a humdinger to keep you up like that."

"I've had bouts of insomnia before. I'm sure that's all this is."

"Try a warm glass of milk."

"Yeah, I will." Tess couldn't tell her roommate she didn't want to go to sleep. She wasn't prepared to explain her nightmare to Delise. But worse, she was afraid Mac would see the dark circles under her eyes and probe for answers. He was much too astute for her peace of mind at times.

When the doorbell rang, Delise hopped to her feet. "I'll get it. Finish your coffee. I wouldn't want you falling asleep on your date."

"It isn't a date. Amy and Johnny are going to be with us."

Delise paused at the doorway. "Sure it isn't. He asked you to go with him. He's picking you up at your apartment. That sounds like a date to me even if the children are chaperoning."

Tess opened her mouth to reply, but Delise fled into the living room. Tess gulped the last few swallows of the lukewarm coffee, rose and put the mug in the sink. When she turned toward the door, Mac stood framed in it, looking incredibly handsome in a pair of blue jeans, faded and worn looking, and a striped red and blue polo shirt. His smile brightened his eyes and sent warmth coursing through her.

"Ready?"

She nodded, not trusting herself to speak. After snatching her purse and a floppy hat to wear in case the sun decided to peek out from behind the clouds, she walked with him to the front door. When she noticed his car was empty, she asked, "Where are Johnny and Amy?"

"Casey picked them up for lunch and a treat. She's bringing them."

"Oh," Tess said, sliding into the passenger side of the car, realizing this felt very much like a date, as Delise had so kindly pointed out.

After he started the car, he threw a quick look at her. "Having trouble sleeping?"

She knew he would say something. Why hadn't she prepared a response? She searched her mind for a reply that wouldn't lead to a lot of questions. None came to mind. "Yes," she finally answered, knowing what his next question would be.

"Why?"

Because I've been dreaming about you getting killed, she thought and gritted her teeth, her gaze trained on the road.

"Another nightmare about Kevin?"

"Yes, I've been having nightmares," she answered, deliberately not elaborating on the subject matter of her dreams.

"Tess, maybe if you talk with Pastor Winthrop, he might be able to help you put the past in perspective."

"Have you completely?"

Mac didn't answer for a moment. "Yes, I think I have. But —" he slid a glance toward her "— I had help. You're trying to do everything by yourself."

"You mean the Lord's help?"

"Yes."

But He's the one who took Kevin away, she wanted to proclaim as she had in the past. Instead she dug her teeth into her lower lip, knowing the truth wasn't that simple. "I'll think about it." That was all she could say.

"That's all I ask." He pulled the car into the church parking lot.

Tess noticed a crowd had formed on the lawn. A large tent offered shelter from the sun, or in this case the rain if the clouds blanketing the sky opened up. People manned the booths under the canvas with

212

various products for sale from food to crafts. Several groups of children were playing games from catch to tag while others romped on the equipment in the playground. Some men milled around the barbecues, talking and peering at the dark sky. To the side of the grills a group of women arranged bowls of food on card tables.

Mac took Tess's hand and led her to the cashier to pay for the evening dinner of hamburgers and hot dogs with an assortment of salads and desserts. She saw several people she knew and waved to Mac's mother behind the table displaying jars of preserved fruit.

"What's the idea of the festival?" Tess asked Mac after he had gotten their meal tickets.

"It's a celebration of people's talents." He gestured to an older lady at the nearest booth. "Ruth loves to knit and makes beautiful sweaters. She sells them every year to help the church raise money. And Candace over there —" he pointed to a young woman who sat in front of an easel "— will draw your portrait for a fee. She's quite good. I'm going to have her do Johnny and Amy."

"Together?"

"Yes. Amy follows Johnny around everywhere. I keep thinking he's gonna get tired of it one day."

"He's never had much of a family. I think Amy's hero-worshiping is a novelty to him." Tess caught Alice motioning for Tess to come over. "Your mother has a booth. Where's yours?"

"Doing what?"

"Well, let's see. You could teach children how to tackle."

"I think that comes naturally."

"You're a good listener. How about a booth where you listen to people?"

"Everyone can listen. That's not a talent."

Tess stopped, standing in Mac's path with one hand on her waist. "Peter MacPherson, being a good listener is very important and something a lot of people don't know how to do. It's a gift that's certainly appreciated by me."

He beamed with a wide grin, his eyes almost silver. "Next year you need to have a clown booth."

Next year. She liked the sound of those words. She returned his smile, feeling her whole face light up. "Yeah, children could throw pies at me."

"Just children?"

The gleam in his eyes made her laugh.

"Maybe little old ladies, too." She started for his mother's booth.

"Can I persuade you to buy some of my preserves? It's like tasting a little bit of heaven with each bite. Want to try a sample?" Alice lavished some blackberry jam onto a piece of toast, then held the plate up.

Tess took a bite of the toast. "Mmm. This is delicious. Do you pick your own fruit?"

"Whenever I can."

"Hey, that's not fair. I want a taste," Mac said, his regard on the toast in Tess's hand.

Without thinking she lifted it to his mouth, and he ate the rest of the sample, his lips grazing her fingertips. Her gaze connected with his as though she were bound to him. The shared moment reinforced the attraction she felt toward Mac.

After a few seconds of silence, Alice coughed, and Tess glanced away from Mac, her face flaming, her legs weak. She gripped the edge of the table to steady herself.

His attention on Tess, Mac said, "Mom, I'll take two of every kind you have."

"At this rate I'll be sold out before the hour's up." Alice began boxing up the jars.

"I'll find the rest of the family and send them over." Mac finally looked at his mother. "Then you can join us at the picnic tables. I'm gonna stake one out for us."

Alice's brow arched. "Just one?"

"You're right, two. Any more and no one else will have one."

Relieved that Mac was no longer staring at her, Tess watched the exchange between mother and son and realized again how much she missed having a family to call her own. "Before you sell out, I'd like to purchase some."

"That's okay, Tess, I bought one for you and one for me." Mac lifted the box from the table.

"But I —"

"Just consider it a thank-you for sending us Johnny. I'm taking this to the car. Be back in a sec."

Mac disappeared through the crowd in the tent before Tess could open her mouth to refuse his gift.

"Hon, one thing I've learned over the years as his mother is to accept the gifts. He loves giving people presents for no reason at all. You're just going to have to get used to it. Besides, this is a donation to the church."

Alice's statement implied Tess would be the recipient of many presents in the future. That thought alarmed her. "He's really become attached to Johnny," Tess said, wanting to steer the conversation away from gifts and anything personal concerning her and Mac. She had always been uncomfortable with people giving her unexpected presents, or even on her birthday and at Christmas.

"He's crazy about the boy."

"What happens if Mrs. Hocks finds a relative?"

Alice shook her head. "It'll break his heart. When I talk with him now, he's always telling me something about Johnny as though the child was his own."

Again Tess thought back to the first day she'd met Mac. She'd been reminded of a gentle bear, and that impression was confirmed the more she was around him.

"He's had several losses in his life. I hope Johnny isn't one of them."

"So do I," Tess murmured, aware that Mac was heading toward them.

Tess followed his progress and noticed several members of the congregation stopping Mac to say something. He drew people to him with his easy ways and warm smile. There was nothing frightening about him even though he was very large and muscularly built. Her gentle bear.

Oh, my! Where had that come from? she wondered and turned her flushed face away before the man read what was in her mind.

She wasn't ready. Was she?

"Let's go find Casey and the kids. See you, Mom, when you're through selling your wares."

When Tess emerged from the tent, she noticed darker clouds rolling in and the smell of rain in the air. A cool breeze picked up, whipping strands of hair about her face. "I think it might rain on this parade."

A drop splattered on top of Mac's head. "Yeah, I think you're right. We'd better get everyone moving indoors to the reception hall."

"But what about all this?" Tess swept her arm toward the tent and the grills set up for preparing dinner.

"I can't complain. We need the rain even if the timing isn't great. The festival will go on, just indoors. We're celebrating our good fortune and the talents God gave us. It doesn't make any difference where that happens."

Thirty minutes later Tess stood in the middle of the large reception hall surrounded by a mass of people crammed inside while thunder sounded and lightning flashed outside. The smiles and laughter attested to the festive atmosphere. Instead of being upset, everyone was glad of the rain, declaring its appropriateness because the children's play was about Noah's ark.

Mac and his brothers helped bring in chairs while Alice and Mary organized some of the churchwomen to prepare the food in the kitchen. Tess suddenly felt the need to escape the press of people. She wasn't sure where she belonged, where her place in this world was. Right now she felt as though she were on the ark in the middle of a sea with no sight of land. Noah found land. Would she?

Tess sought refuge in the sanctuary where the loud sounds of the festival were muffled by the thick, heavy double doors and walls of stone. Several soft lights illuminated the church in a warm glow of welcome. She walked toward the front and sat in a pew. The simple cross on the altar drew her attention. Staring at it, she thought of what Christ had done for mankind the day He had died on the cross. Slowly as her mind replayed Jesus's message, peace washed through her, cleansing her soul, erasing the guilt she'd carried around for so long.

She closed her eyes and listened to the sounds of the rain battering the roof of the sanctuary and sensed a feeling of safety, as if nothing could touch her inside these four walls. She hadn't experienced that in years, especially since the day in the Andes when her life had changed, when men had come down from the mountains and taken something precious from her. Now she realized she had allowed those men to rob her of not just Kevin, but her faith, as well. She had turned her back on the Lord when she should have been embracing Him, letting Him fully into her life to heal the gaping wound.

"Our Father, please give me the strength to see Your plan for me. Help me to open my heart to You again and to forgive myself for living when so many died. I can't do it alone anymore. I need You."

After setting up the chairs for the play, Mac searched the reception hall for Tess. When he didn't find her, he checked the kitchen, then went back into the hall.

"I saw her go into the sanctuary." Casey came up to Mac.

"Her?"

"Don't try to pretend you don't know who I'm talking about. I saw you looking for Tess. When she isn't with you, you're always searching for her in the crowd."

"And what's that supposed to mean?"

"You're falling hard for her." Casey lifted her chin a notch as though to challenge her brother to deny what she said.

"Tess and I are friends. We —"

His sister placed her hands on her hips and shot him a disgruntled look. "Mac, quit fooling yourself. You've never done that before, so why start now."

"I'm trying to help her."

"Oh, good grief, Mac, get real. You are interested in Tess Morgan, and it goes way beyond friendship."

"You said she went into the sanctuary?" Mac asked, deciding to ignore his little sister's observation. She was only nineteen and had a lot to learn about the world.

"Yes."

Mac headed for the church but paused at the double doors. Why had Tess gone inside? To speak with God? Should he disturb her? He looked around the quiet foyer, trying to decide what he should do. One of the doors opened. He stepped back.

Tess emerged from the sanctuary, a calm serenity touching her beautiful features as though the Lord had touched her. Her eyes glowed with an inner light when she peered at him. The smile that graced her lips melted his irritation at his sister.

"The most wonderful thing happened to me." Tess grasped his hands. "I talked with the Lord and He heard me." Tears welled up in her eyes and flowed down her cheeks. "Oh, Mac, you were so right. I should never have turned away from God when Kevin died. I should have turned to Him."

Mac took her into his arms and held her close to his heart. The pressure in his chest constricted his breathing. A lump lodged in his throat, and he had to swallow several times before he could speak. "I'm so glad you realize the Lord hasn't abandoned you."

She leaned back, her arms loosely about him. "But I abandoned the Lord."

"Remember the story of the shepherd leaving his flock to look for the lost sheep? He has found you and taken you back into the flock."

Through the shimmer of tears Tess regarded Mac, the tenderness she saw deep in his eyes. Emotions bombarded her from all sides, leaving her feeling drained but content. If it hadn't been for this man, she might never have found her way back to the Lord. She owed Mac a lot. Certainly her loyalty and friendship, but could she give him her love?

He held her face in his large hands. "You're special to the Lord and you're special to —"

"Mac, Tess, the play is about to start."

Tess shifted quickly away from Mac and turned toward Johnny, who rushed toward them. "Are you ready?"

"Yep, I've got my lines memorized. I've been helping Amy with hers."

"Do you need any help getting your costume on?"

"No, Casey's helping Amy then she's gonna help me." Johnny grabbed Tess's hand. "Come on. I want you two sitting in the front row. I had Mrs. MacPherson save you places."

"Okay, we're coming, buddy."

After Tess sat between Alice and Mac, she glanced down the row of chairs and saw all the MacPhersons. Tess felt honored to be included in the family event. All the children were in the play, with Johnny portraying Noah and Amy the white dove that found land.

"I wish we could open up the skylight and let the rain in. Then we would really have an authentic backdrop for the play," Alice whispered as the youth director came on stage to quiet the audience.

Mac leaned around Tess and replied, "I think we should just have it out in the parking lot."

A streak of lightning crackled the air followed by a loud boom that rocked the room.

"I think I prefer staying indoors," Tess said, staring at the storm raging outside the window.

Amy shot out from behind the curtain on the stage and rushed to Mac, throwing herself into his lap and burying her face against his shirt. "Daddy, I don't like this," the little girl mumbled against him.

Another flash of light lit the darkened room, immediately accompanied by the sound of thunder. "Sweetheart, that's just the Lord shouting His joy to the world. If it didn't rain, life on Earth would cease to be."

"But, Daddy, it's so loud." She clapped her hands over her ears as thunder reverberated through the hall again.

"That's so everyone will be able to hear even from far away," Mac said when Amy cautiously uncovered her ears, her eyes round as saucers.

"It's just the Lord?"

"Yes, pumpkin. The sound won't hurt you."

She sat for a moment longer, her head cocked as she listened to the thunder rumble again. "You're right, Daddy. It doesn't hurt."

Mac hugged Amy. "You'd better get back behind stage. You're the most important part of this play."

Amy puffed out her chest. "I'm the one who finds land." She hopped from his lap and raced for the stage.

Tess touched Mac's hand. "I've always hated storms, too. Now I'll never think of them any other way than God's celebration of life."

"He does in many ways, small and large. It's all around us, Tess. The birth of a child. A new day."

"The miracle of love. A parent and child's love is a wonderful testament to the Lord."

The rest of the world faded from Mac's view. All his senses centered on the feel of her hand over his, of her scent of lilacs, of her beautiful features radiating with her renewed faith in the Lord. "Not just a love between a parent and child. There are all kinds of love. Each important in God's plan. Jesus's message to us was based on God's love for us."

Tears made her eyes glisten. "I'm just now rediscovering that."

So am I, Mac thought, sandwiching her hand between his. Was he brave enough to pursue this to the end? To discover what God had in mind for him and Tess?

Chapter Eleven

"Don't be ridiculous. I don't mind taking you home." Tess braked at a stoplight and sent Casey a reassuring look.

"My car didn't start this morning."

"Cars, like computers, are wonderful until they don't work." Tess came to a stop at another light, scanning the intersection, the billboard —

In big, red letters, a message was written for all the world, or at least the people of Denver, to see. Tess, Will You Go With Me To The Circus Tonight? Yours, Mac. Her cheeks flamed the color of the letters.

"Your car isn't broken, is it?" Tess asked, aware the driver behind her was honking at her because the light was green and she hadn't moved. She pressed her foot on the accelerator, gunning through the intersection.

"I never said it was broken. I said it didn't start this morning. That's because I didn't try to start it. Mac brought me to work so I could get a ride home with you."

Tess's face still felt hot. "Why didn't he just call me up and ask me himself?"

Casey shrugged. "Not sure. You can ask him yourself. He's right there."

Tess pulled into Alice's driveway and saw the man in question leaning against his car with his arms folded over his chest and a pleased grin on his face. "I think I'll do just that."

When she approached him, the twinkle in his eyes erased any embarrassment she might have felt. After all, she wasn't the only one in Denver who went by the name of Tess, and surely there were lots of Macs who lived in the city. "I could be busy."

"Are you?" He lifted one brow.

"I should be, since you waited until the last minute to ask."

"I checked with Casey, and she said you weren't."

Tess frowned, remembering Casey drilling her yesterday about her plans for the week, including this evening.

"I wanted to surprise you. Do something different that you wouldn't expect."

"You got me there. I didn't expect the billboard or the circus."

"Amy and Johnny are coming, too. How about it?"

"You know I won't say no when you mention them," she said in an accusing voice that didn't sound very strong.

"A guy will use any means to get a gal to go out with him."

"You're that desperate?"

"You bet, where you're concerned. You've turned me down in the past."

"Not for a long time."

"In football I learned to anticipate every move of my opponent."

"Now I'm an opponent. That doesn't bode well for the date."

He chuckled. "I think this date will go just fine. You can call it research."

"Research? For what?"

"For your clown therapy, what else? There are gonna be a lot of clowns at the circus."

"Oh, so this was purely for my benefit?"

His easy laughter filled the air. "Hardly. Definitely it's for my benefit — and the children's, of course."

"You certainly know how to hit below the belt. You know how much I love being with Amy and Johnny."

"I hope not just them." His gray eyes glittered with that twinkle.

"No, not just them."

The air between them crackled with a

finely honed tension. Their gazes remained bound while the world continued around them. One minute slid into two, yet Tess couldn't find the strength to walk to her car.

Finally Mac straightened as though suddenly remembering they were standing on a public street with only a few hours until their date. "I'll pick you up at six. Be ready to eat a lot of junk food and to have some fun."

Tess saluted. "Aye, aye, sir."

His chuckles drifted to her as she strolled to her car and climbed in. Something was in the air. She felt the charged atmosphere as though it were a palpable force. As she neared her apartment, her excitement grew. Their relationship was evolving to another level. She was no longer denying her attraction, and neither was he.

Tess stuffed the last of the chili dog into her mouth, chewed the gooey mess, then licked her lips. "My arteries won't thank you, but I do."

"Here, you missed some chili." Mac dabbed a paper napkin on her chin.

His gaze captured hers. Again, her surroundings faded and all her senses were centered on Mac — so close that he threatened her equilibrium. Because of him, she looked forward to each new day. She had rediscovered the Lord and her faith. Mac had become very important in her life.

She blinked, shattering the moment of connection. "I love these things, but they aren't easy to eat," she said to cover her disconcerting revelation.

Amy peered at her father. "When are the clowns coming out?"

Tess took one look at the little girl with chili smeared all over her face and grinned. "It's contagious."

She took a napkin and cleaned Amy. As she wiped the child's chin, Tess couldn't shake the feeling she wanted to do this more often, on a regular basis. The knowledge left her shaken.

A man mounted the steps into the stands, selling cotton candy. Pulling on Mac's arm, Johnny asked, "Can I have some?"

"That's pure sugar."

"I know. That's why I love it."

"Why did I bother saying that?" Mac muttered to Tess and raised his hand to ask the man to pass down two cotton candies.

"A parent's duty is to be a voice of reason." Tess shoved the newfound emotions concerning Mac and Amy away to be examined in the privacy of her apartment. When Mac pulled out some money and paid for the cotton candies, Tess asked, "What about me?"

"You, too?" Mac signaled for another one.

"Afraid so. I have a big sweet tooth I try to keep under control."

"You're not succeeding."

"Nope." Tess took the cotton candy Mac handed her.

"Your dentist must love you."

"I don't have one cavity in my mouth."

He shot her a surprised glance right before the music swelled and the ringmaster announced the clowns.

"Daddy, look!" Amy pointed at a clown who had curly red hair and a big frown painted on his face.

He came running out and tripped over his large shoes, falling facedown in the arena. Two more bounded out, stumbled over the same imaginary spot, landing in a heap on top of the first one. Everyone in the audience laughed as the clowns tried to stand and ended up in a jumbled mess.

Halfway through their routine, Mac leaned across Amy and whispered to Tess, "Getting any ideas?"

"These skits require at least two people. Are you volunteering to get drenched with a bottle of water?"

"Since you're helping me at the halfway house, I guess I could help you if it doesn't involve putting on makeup. I have an image to uphold."

"I'll have to remember that the next time I'm entertaining the children on the floor."

His eyes sparkled with humor. "I'm gonna be up there day after tomorrow. I think I could manage being a straight man."

"Shh, Daddy, I can't hear."

"Sorry, pumpkin."

Tess tried to contain her smile, but every time she peered at Mac she pictured him with water dripping off his face. The wonderful part of that picture would be Mac's laughter. He enjoyed life.

"Somehow I get the feeling you aren't grinning about the performance," Mac whispered.

Pressing her lips in a straight line, Tess focused her attention on the center ring, but she felt Mac's gaze on her. She resisted the strong urge to look at him again. When the clown routine was over, she realized she couldn't remember a single thing any clown had done. All her thoughts were fixed on the mischievous gleam in Mac's eyes.

When a couple of performers traversed the high wire on a bicycle, Johnny exclaimed with wide eyes, "I'd like to try that."

232

"Not without years of experience behind you," Mac immediately said. "Promise?"

Johnny nodded. "I didn't mean I would."

"How about me, Daddy?"

"Same goes for you. It isn't something to try at home. Understand, Amy?"

"I wouldn't. I don't like high places."

Mac sighed heavily. "I think that's one fear I'm glad she has."

At the end of the performance Johnny jumped to his feet and clapped. Amy quickly followed suit, pumping her arm in the air like Johnny. Tess realized in a short time Mac had made Johnny feel like a part of the family. For a few seconds she thought about him as a father — of her children. Quickly she pushed that from her mind but not before she acknowledged he would be an excellent one.

As they climbed down the stands, Amy took Tess and Johnny's hands. Mac linked his fingers through Tess's. Together — like a real family — they made their way through the crowd to the car.

When everyone was settled inside, Mac pulled out of the parking space. "Come back to the house with us. It's still early. I thought we could play a game, then put the children to bed. After that I'll take you home."

The scene he described fueled the image

of being a family in Tess's mind. Its temptation enticed her to accept. "I can't stay up too late. I work tomorrow."

"One game."

"I want to play Twister," Amy said.

"Yeah," Johnny added.

"Then Twister it is."

"I'm gonna spin for everyone," Amy said with a shout of joy. "I do that real good."

Thirty minutes later Tess contorted her body to reach a yellow circle with her right hand.

Amy spun the wheel for her father. "Red, Daddy."

Mac twisted to look at the spinner, then plopped his left foot in the circle next to Tess. His face was inches from hers. Chuckling, he tickled Tess in the side, causing her to fall forward into Johnny, who managed to plow into Amy on the sideline. Mac jumped back, avoiding the pile of arms and legs, laughing at the sight of the entwined body parts before him.

"This reminds me of the clowns at the circus," he said, trying to bring his laughter under control.

Tess looked up. "I think it's payback time, kids." Pulling her arm free from the bottom of the heap, she rose, her gaze fixed on Mac with mischief in mind.

He began to back up, his hands out to ward off the advancing trio. "I'm sure in the rules somewhere it states no ganging up."

"I can't read, Daddy."

"Mac, it says nothing of the sort." Tess proceeded toward him with Johnny on one side and Amy on the other.

"Well, it should. It's highly unfair."

"And tickling an opponent is fair?"

Mac feinted a move to the right, then circled the group. Tess lunged toward his upper body at the same time the two children went for his legs. Mac went down with a thump. Sitting on her haunches, Tess let Amy and Johnny tickle Mac in the ribs. His laughter warmed her insides, confirming the feeling of closeness she'd had all evening.

"Uncle. Uncle," Mac called.

Reluctantly the children stopped, but Amy flung herself at her father, wrapping her arms around his neck.

"This has been the bestest day." The little girl kissed Mac's cheek.

"Yeah. I've never been to the circus," Johnny added.

"I'm glad you two enjoyed it. Now it's time for bed."

"Can't we stay up a little later?"

"No." Mac sat up, bringing Amy with

him. "You two get ready and I'll be in to say good-night."

"Tess, too?" Amy asked.

"I wouldn't miss it for the world."

With slumped shoulders and bent heads, the two children left the room. Tess sat on the floor near Mac with her legs tucked against her chest and her arms wrapped around them.

"They're quite good at trying to make me feel bad that they have to go to bed," Mac said with a chuckle. "Apparently Johnny didn't have a bedtime before coming here. You should have heard him the first night I told him it was time to go to sleep. Amy has since learned to do the same thing. The other day she told me she would be four soon and perfectly capable of staying up all night. That was said with her arms folded and her chin tilted as though daring me to deny the fact."

"Has she picked up any other habits from Johnny that you've had to contend with?"

"A few, but Johnny has been so good for Amy. She's quick to share her things with him. She doesn't even mind when I pay Johnny some extra attention. That worried me at first. She's thrilled to have him here."

"Have you heard from Mrs. Hocks about her search?"

The lines in his forehead deepened. He rose and began to pace as though nervous and not sure what to do with the extra energy. "Not in a few days. I have to confess I've started praying that she isn't successful. I don't want Johnny to leave here."

"Hopefully things will work out."

Mac stopped in the middle of the den and faced her, his arms straight at his sides. "What if they don't and Johnny has to leave?"

"Then you will deal with it. You're one of the strongest men I know. Your faith will sustain you."

Mac knelt in front of Tess and took her hands. "But when I think about the possibility —"

Tess pressed her fingers over his mouth to stop his flow of words. "Shh. Don't borrow trouble."

Mac's gaze snared hers and held it for a long moment. He started to lean forward when Amy called that she was ready for bed. "I guess that's our cue." Rising, he towered over Tess and offered his hand to help her to her feet.

"And I need to get home after I say goodnight to Amy and Johnny." Tess tamped her disappointment. She'd wanted Mac to kiss her.

"That long day tomorrow?" Mac asked while they walked down the hallway.

Tess nodded and entered Amy's room. She sat in her white canopy bed with scores of books scattered over her pink bedspread.

"Daddy, I want you to read this one and this one and —"

"One, Amy, at bedtime. You know the rule."

She screwed her features into a thoughtful look and flipped through the books until she found the one she wanted. "Can Tess read it to me tonight?"

"Sure." Mac slid a glance toward Tess. "If she wants to."

"Are you kidding? I would be honored to read you a story."

Amy scooted over and made room for Tess. "Great."

"What about your prayers?"

Amy folded her hands and bowed her head. "Our Father, please watch over Daddy, Johnny, Grandma, Tess, Nina and all my uncles, aunts and cousins. Thank you for a great time at the circus. Amen."

When Tess heard her name included in the list of people Amy wanted God to protect, her throat closed. It took a moment after the child finished her prayer to feel her voice was strong enough to read to Amy.

Finally Tess began the story about a princess who was lost and trying to find her way home. By the time she came to the end and looked at Amy, the little girl was asleep, her head resting against Tess's arm. She closed the book and carefully slid off the bed while Mac shifted Amy to a more comfortable position then covered her with a blanket.

At the door Tess glanced at the child, the soft glow of the night-light illuminating her angelic face. She wanted children. Seeing Amy sleeping so peacefully underscored her desire for a family. For the first time in a long while she began to wonder if it might be possible for her dream to come true. Walking with Mac toward Johnny's room heightened the possibility in her mind. Mac is a wonderful father, she thought. She knew he had expressed reservations about having any more children, but surely if the right woman came along he would change his mind. Just because his wife had died giving birth didn't mean it would happen again. She hoped she could get him to see that.

When Tess entered Johnny's bedroom, she saw he was already asleep. Disappointment washed over her.

Mac switched off the lamp beside the boy's bed. "He still hasn't been able to manage staying up much later than Amy."

"It'll take a while for his strength to return completely. I'm pleased to see him doing so much," Tess whispered, making her way to the bedroom door.

"He's been pretty good about not overextending himself. I haven't had to say much at all to him about slowing down."

"He has a lot to offer."

"I'm hoping he's beginning to realize that."

"How could he not with you as the teacher, Mac? He's lucky you came into his life."

"I was thinking the same thing about myself. I needed Johnny. It was my lucky day when I discovered you crying in the waiting room."

The sincerity in his voice nearly undid her composure. "I think it's worked out for everyone." She started for the den, tired from the long day at work and content from the evening spent with Mac and the children.

He took her hand, and Tess found herself leaning into his strength, desperately trying not to yawn. His arm came up to cradle her close to him as she continued making her way toward the den.

"I'll drive you home before you fall asleep on me."

She did yawn then. "It isn't your company, I assure you." She laid her head on his shoulder.

"I know, Tess Morgan. I've seen you working. If I ever got sick, I'd like you to be my nurse."

"When was the last time you were sick?" She bent and snatched her purse from the floor by the couch.

"Not counting my broken leg —" he scratched his head "— you know, I can't remember. I've never had to stay in the hospital except that time I had my appendix out, and besides a few football injuries, I haven't been sick."

"Then it looks like my services won't be needed," she said with a laugh. "Thankfully, since men are lousy patients."

"Oh, I'm wounded." Mac clasped a hand over his heart. "Is that the female or the nurse in you saying that?"

She winked at him as she walked from the room. "I'm not telling."

"Colt, what brings you to the hospital?" Tess asked as she saw the big man approach the nurses' station.

"Me." Casey came up behind Tess and put a folder on the counter. "I found a collie mix the other day. I thought Colt's farm would be the perfect place for him to stay while I find him a home. Mom told me only one pet allowed at our place."

"I was coming to town so I offered to pick the dog up," Colt added quickly.

Tess looked from Casey to Colt and noticed a flush in her cheeks. Colt was shifting from one foot to the other. Tess realized Casey had taken the children to the farm a few weekends before. She had said because Johnny and Amy had begged her. Now Tess wondered if the kids had begged very much.

"I see," Tess said, taking the folder from the counter and preparing to leave them alone.

"We thought we would stop by Mac's and say hi, maybe go out for some pizza, all of us. Want to come along?" Casey asked, keeping her gaze averted from Colt's.

"I wouldn't want to intrude on —"

Colt dismissed her concerns with a wave of his hand. "You wouldn't be. Johnny and Amy love pizza, and I thought it would be fun for all of us to go to dinner, including you. Besides, what would Mac do if you didn't come along?"

It was Tess's turn to blush. She started to say something and realized she had no reply. The implication of what Colt had said thrilled her and scared her. Did the world think of them as a couple? Did Mac think of them as a couple? She and Mac had spent a lot of time together in the past few months. She had always told herself that they spent time together because of the children. She'd been lying to herself. She wanted them to be a couple.

"I guess I could. I need to go by my apartment first and change. After being in these all day, I'm ready to change." She gestured to her pastel green pants and shirt with small rainbows splashed all over them.

"Then we'll meet you over at his house." Casey retrieved her sweater from the back of her chair.

"Does Mac know you're coming?"

"No, but then that's part of the fun, surprising him. He expects it from me. Don't worry. By the time you get there, he'll know about the plans we have for him." Casey sauntered toward the elevator with Colt next to her.

Tess pulled up behind the row of cars in Mac's circular driveway, the sun heading down toward the mountains. Casey opened the front door.

"Sorry, it took me longer than I expected. Rush hour traffic is a bear today."

"Yeah, I know. We only arrived a few

minutes ago ourselves."

"Where are the children?" Tess stepped into the large foyer.

"In the backyard showing off their puppies to Colt. Mac's out there, too." Casey added the last sentence with a gleam sparkling in her eyes as though to say she knew that Tess really wanted to know where Mac was. "And he's thrilled about this impromptu dinner, especially when he heard you were coming along."

"You know I noticed how close you were to Colt when you left work," Tess said as she walked next to Casey toward the back of the house.

"Just friends."

Tess glanced at Casey, realizing that was exactly what she had been telling everyone about her and Mac. "Sure. Keep telling yourself that. There are plenty of good shelters for animals in a city this size, I'm sure. Why did you call Colt about the dog?"

"A collie needs lots of room to run around." Casey fired the words back.

"And Colt dropped everything to come into Denver, an hour's drive, to pick up the dog from you." Tess reached for the handle of the back door.

"Okay. I won't say another word about you and Mac. But Tess, before I clam up, I just have to say I haven't seen my big brother this happy in a long time. You make him laugh."

"Must be the clown in me."

Casey stopped her from going out. "Does he make you laugh?"

Tess grew serious. "Yes."

Nodding in satisfaction, Casey smiled. "Good. Then I leave the rest in the Lord's hands."

In the back yard Johnny threw a ball to Frisky. The puppy chased it, stumbling over her own big feet. Buttons pounced on the ball, which set the two puppies fighting over it.

Amy put her hand on her waist. "I've been trying to teach them to share."

Mac laughed. "Honey, that'll take time. They are only a few months old."

The puppies tumbled until Frisky managed to take the ball and dart off with it. Buttons bounded to her feet and went after her sister.

Amy huffed, starting for the two puppies who were again vying for the ball. "They're family. They shouldn't fight so much. Johnny and me don't."

Mac saw Tess and strolled over to her with a smile in his eyes. "I'm glad you could come. The children are so excited about going out for pizza. You would think I don't feed them."

Tess leaned close to Mac to whisper, "Don't tell them, but so am I. I know pizza is mega calories a slice but I love it, too."

"Your secret is safe with me — for a price."

Tess arched a brow. "What?"

"That you come back with us and help me get the kids to bed. They don't put up a big argument when you're here. The other night was a breeze compared to most."

The idea of helping him put the children to bed pleased her. She felt a fluttering in her stomach, as though butterflies were beating their wings against her. "Sure. I can't pass up a chance to read another story to Amy."

"I doubt it'll be another story. She's been stuck on that one for the past two weeks. She could probably recite it to you."

Nina opened the back door and called to Mac. He jogged over to her and listened, his face tensing into a frown, the taut set of his shoulders indicating displeasure.

When he came back he said, "Mrs. Hocks is here to see me about Johnny. Will you come with me?"

"Have you said anything to her about wanting to adopt Johnny?"

"I called her this morning, but she was out of the office. Maybe this is her way of returning my call." He kneaded the back of his neck, his forehead creased in a frown. "Still, I've got this feeling —" He let the rest of his sentence fade into silence.

"Do you think something is wrong?" Tension vibrated from him, making Tess tighten her muscles until they ached.

"She's dropped by before unexpectedly, but — Oh, it's nothing. I'll feel better when I can get the proceedings started on the adoption." Mac called over his shoulder to the group in the yard, "Be back in a minute."

Casey and Colt were deep in conversation and barely acknowledged their departure. Johnny and Amy were busy chasing after their puppies and rolling around in the grass with them. Tess glimpsed the beautiful family scene and shuddered, Mac's worries becoming her worries.

Mrs. Hocks stood in the middle of the living room, staring out the picture window. She clasped her purse in one hand and a notebook in the other. When she heard them enter, she pivoted toward them with a smile on her face.

"I've got good news."

Tess felt Mac relax next to her, his features easing into his own smile of greeting.

"And I have good news, too," he said, beckoning for Mrs. Hocks to have a seat on the couch while he and Tess sat across from her on the other one. "What's yours?"

"I found a relative of Johnny's this afternoon who lives in California."

Without taking his gaze from the child welfare worker, Mac fumbled for Tess's hand and grasped it.

"Dottie Brown is his father's sister. She's coming to pick Johnny up. She didn't know about Johnny's mother's death. She lost touch with them a few years back. So isn't it great that Johnny will finally be with his family?" Mrs. Hocks beamed, delighted with her accomplishment.

The silence following her announcement pulsated with tension. Mac's grip tightened on Tess's fingers. The sides of the lady's mouth fell as she looked from Mac to Tess then back to Mac.

"I thought you would be happy."

Mac swallowed hard, a muscle in his jaw twitching. "And she wants to adopt him?"

"She's coming to Denver. She hasn't said yes yet, but I think she will. She hasn't seen Johnny in six years." Mrs. Hocks peered toward the entrance. "I wanted to tell Johnny about his aunt. Where is he?"

"He's out back playing with his puppy."

Mrs. Hocks started to stand.

"Wait," Mac said, halting the woman, who immediately eased down on the couch. "I'd prefer telling him, if that's all right with you."

"Well, I guess so."

Mac rose. "When should he be ready to meet his aunt?"

"Day after tomorrow. I'll bring her to the house in the afternoon. Have Johnny's things packed." Mrs. Hocks came to her feet, her brow wrinkled. "What good news did you have?"

Mac shrugged. "Nothing really. The doctor said he's still in remission and everything looks good."

"Great! That will certainly ease his aunt's mind."

Mac escorted Mrs. Hocks to the front door, then returned to the living room where Tess remained, stunned by the news. The anguish on his face when he entered said it all. She could feel his devastation even before he drew her to him and held her tight. It mirrored what she was experiencing.

"I know I shouldn't have, but I was beginning to think of Johnny as my son. What am I going to do?" He trembled with the force of his pain.

Mac's question tore her heart into pieces. There were no words to comfort him, to take his anguish away. Then she remembered the words of the twenty-third Psalm and began reciting them. She emphasized the words, "Yea, though I walk through the valley of the shadow of death, I will fear no evil: for Thou art with me; Thy rod and Thy staff they comfort me."

Listening to her softly spoken words, Mac drew in a deep, calming breath, then another. He pulled back and stared at her, his hands framing her face. "You're right. The Lord will guide me."

"Tell Mrs. Hocks your desire to adopt Johnny. Maybe it will make a difference. Maybe his aunt doesn't want to adopt him."

Resting his forehead against hers, Mac tunneled his fingers through her hair. "I love Johnny, but I can't deny him his true family for my selfish needs."

Tess gripped his forearms. "Don't say that. You're not selfish. You took him into your home and gave him a family when he needed it the most, when no one else wanted him. There was nothing selfish about that."

He gathered her again to him, so close she could feel his heart pounding. Its slow, tormented beat passed into her body, matching the rhythm of hers.

"Johnny may not want to go with his aunt. Have you thought about that?"

"Yes, but I can't influence him unduly. I have to give it a chance to work for Johnny. Family is important."

"Family is more than a mere blood relationship."

Mac sighed. "It would have been so much easier if Mrs. Hocks hadn't found any relatives."

"Life doesn't always follow the easy path."

"I know, but that doesn't stop me from wishing it would." He straightened away from Tess, shadows in his eyes. "God only puts what we can handle before us. We'd better return to our guests before they begin to wonder."

"Are you kidding! Johnny and Amy are too busy playing with their puppies, and in case you haven't noticed, Colt and Casey are too busy having eyes only for each other."

Tess walked beside Mac, his hand in hers. His earlier words about God only giving them what they could deal with made her take another look at what had happened to her in South America. She was a stronger person because of the tragedy, and with her recent return to the Lord, each day her faith grew. She realized that He had spared her because He had plans for her.

"Tess, don't say anything. I want to tell Johnny about his aunt after dinner. I don't want to spoil this evening."

"I'm not very good at acting."

"Neither am I, but we have to. It's important."

She squeezed his hand. "I know."

The minute Mac stepped outside, Amy ran up to him. "Daddy, I'm hungry. Can we go eat now?"

He scooped her into his arms and hugged her tightly to him. "Of course, pumpkin. Where do you want to go for pizza?"

"Bear Country."

"I don't know why I bother asking." Shaking his head, he rolled his eyes. "That's the only place she wants to go out to eat. She loves the dancing bears, but her favorite part of the show is the singing chipmunk that pops up from the log. She laughs every time he performs."

" 'Cause he's funny, Daddy."

"We can all pile into my car if you all don't mind close quarters," Mac said to the group.

Tess noticed his big grin, but she hoped she was the only one who saw the dull flatness to his eyes. This would be a difficult evening, but she was determined to stay as long as he needed her.

After the children put their puppies in the utility room, everyone crammed into Mac's vehicle. Colt and Casey didn't seem to mind being crunched together in the back with Amy in her car seat. The close quarters in front allowed Tess to place her arm around Johnny.

Fifteen minutes later they arrived at Bear Country Pizza House where loud noises during the shows made it almost impossible for any conversation to take place. Thankfully the next show wasn't starting for another twenty minutes.

After everyone gave their order to the waitress, Amy hopped down from her booster chair. "I want to ride the helicopter. Can Johnny take me?"

"Sure, if he doesn't mind." While Johnny stood, Mac dug into his pocket for some quarters and came up with a fist full. "You two split this. The pizzas should be here in fifteen minutes."

Johnny took the money, then Amy's hand and they headed for the arcade area of the restaurant. Mac kept an eye on the pair as they went from ride to ride, his smile no longer on his face, the feelings he was

253

holding at bay clearly visible in his eyes.

"Okay, I can tell something's wrong, big brother. 'Fess up."

"Mrs. Hocks found Johnny's aunt."

"That's gre—" Casey narrowed her gaze on Mac. "That isn't great. I thought that was what everyone was waiting for."

Mac peered at his sister for a few seconds before swinging his attention to the children. "I've come to think of Johnny as part of our family."

"Oh, Mac." Casey reached out and patted her brother's hand. "I'm sorry."

"Here they come. Not a word. Johnny doesn't know, and I don't want anything to ruin this dinner."

While the children settled into their seats, the waitress brought their pizzas. Mac said a quick blessing just as the show started. Loud music sounded from the speakers not too far from their table, drowning out all conversation.

Taking a slice with Canadian bacon and extra cheese, Tess watched the show while forcing herself to eat at least some pizza. But her food settled in her stomach like a rock and her heart wasn't in the fun songs and silly jokes. She tried to laugh at all the appropriate places, but she was sure anyone paying close attention could see the strain about her mouth and hear the brittleness in her laugh.

By the time they left the pizza parlor, Tess felt her nerves stretched to their limit and her stomach muscles constricted into a tight ball. A glance at Mac confirmed he was experiencing the same thing. Even Casey didn't chatter on the ride to Mac's house.

Tess knew Johnny suspected something when Mac said goodbye to his sister and friend, then asked Johnny and Amy to come into the den. The boy dragged his feet down the hall, and worry nibbled at his expression as he plopped down on the couch across from Mac.

"Did the doctor call or something? I feel fine. Honest." Johnny folded his arms across his stomach and got that defiant look on his face that had all but disappeared in the past weeks at Mac's.

"No, Johnny. You're still in remission. You're doing everything you're supposed to."

"Then what's wrong?"

"Mrs. Hocks came this afternoon to see me about you." Mac paused, cleared his throat, then continued, "She found your aunt, Dottie Brown."

"I don't remember her."

"She remembers you and is coming to see

you the day after tomorrow."

Mac forced a light tone, but Tess could see the anguish each word caused. A nerve in his jaw jerked, and his hands were clasped together so tightly Tess could see his white knuckles.

"Why?" Johnny's defiant look wavered.

"She wants you to come live with her."

Johnny shot off the couch, his hands clenched at his sides. "I don't want to live with no stranger. I don't remember her."

"Perhaps when you see her —"

"No!" Johnny shouted and raced from the room.

"Daddy? Daddy, don't send Johnny away." Tears rolled down Amy's cheeks. "I don't want him to go. Please."

Mac held his arms out for Amy. "Honey, Dottie Brown is Johnny's family."

Amy ignored her father's outstretched arms. "No, we are." She ran from the room, her sobs echoing in the silence.

Mac dropped his arms to his lap. "I don't want him to go, either," he whispered, all the pain he felt lacing each word.

Chapter Twelve

The doorbell sounded in the stillness like a death toll. Mac stiffened. On the couch, Amy grabbed Johnny's hand and held tight. Tess felt the beat of her heart pick up and thunder in her ears.

Mac signaled Nina to remain seated, then surged to his feet on the second chime, his features set in a neutral expression that Tess knew cost him dearly to maintain. The rigid set to his stance attested to the real emotions underlying his facade.

"She's here," Amy whispered so loudly she might as well have shouted the news.

Tess wanted to go to Johnny and scoop him into her arms. She wanted to declare to Mrs. Hocks and Dottie Brown that Johnny was perfectly happy where he was. Instead, Tess remained seated in the wing chair across from the boy, there for support for Johnny, Mac and Amy. This whole day, members of Mac's family had stopped by to see Johnny and say their goodbyes. Several times Tess had seen the boy nearly break down in tears, but somehow he pulled himself together with that stalwart expression that was on his face now as though nothing could touch him. Tess knew otherwise. She had been there herself and felt his pain as if it were her own.

Johnny watched as Mrs. Hocks and his aunt entered the den. Amy's gaze widened, and she leaned closer to him.

Tess forced a smile of greeting that quivered at the corners of her mouth and disappeared almost as quickly as it appeared. "Good day, Mrs. Hocks."

"Tess, it's good to see you," the older woman said.

Mac came in behind the two ladies, his eyes dark gray. "Johnny, do you have everything?"

The boy nodded but didn't move.

"Johnny, this is your aunt Dottie." Mrs. Hocks gestured to the woman next to her.

Dottie moved to the end of the couch, her expression restrained as she took in her nephew. "It's been a while since we last saw each other. Are you ready to go?"

Johnny looked toward Mac, and for a fleeting moment desperation edged its way into the boy's eyes before he masked his feelings behind his world-weary expression.

"Where's your suitcase?" his aunt asked.

Johnny pointed to several black pieces sitting near the doorway.

"Then we'd better get going. I'm sure these good people have things they need to do."

"Oh, no. We don't want Johnny to leave," Amy exclaimed, her body pressed against his side, her hand on his arm as though that would keep him there.

"Amy, we've talked about this."

"But, Daddy, we don't."

Mac positioned himself behind the couch and clamped his hands on Amy's shoulders while she released her grip on the boy. "Johnny, do you want me to help you with your stuff?"

"Yes, please." The boy jumped to his feet and raced from the room.

"Where's he going?" Dottie asked, alarmed at her nephew's sudden move.

"He probably forgot something," Mac said, taking Amy's hand and walking to the luggage.

Johnny reappeared a minute later with Frisky in his arms. "I'm ready to leave."

"A puppy?" Alarmed, Dottie looked at Mrs. Hocks. "You didn't say anything about a puppy. I —"

"I'll take real good care of Frisky."

Johnny held the animal cradled against his chest, his face buried in her fur. "Won't I, Nina? She never has to clean up after Frisky."

Nina cleared her throat, started to say something, then instead, nodded, a sheen to her eyes. She spun away, pretending an interest in something on the coffee table.

Doubt clouded his aunt's expression. "We'll try her tonight and see."

Relieved, Johnny kissed his puppy's head, fighting the tears threatening him. For a long moment everyone just stared at the boy, the silence in the room deafening.

"Let's go," Mrs. Hocks said, the sound unusually loud.

Johnny took a step back and came up against Mac.

He laid a reassuring hand on the boy's shoulder, leaned down and said, "Don't forget to write. When you get settled, we'll call you."

Johnny nodded, his lower lip trembling.

"May I have a word with you, Mr. MacPherson, in private?" Dottie asked.

"You all go ahead." Mac motioned toward the children, Nina and Mrs. Hocks. "Tess, stay please."

Both Amy and Johnny hesitated.

"I'll just be a minute."

The children followed Mrs. Hocks and Nina from the room, leaving the three adults to face each other. Tess felt the tension emanating from Mac in waves and wished she could take his pain away.

"I want to thank you for taking care of my nephew. I also want to ask you not to call him. Let him settle in and get used to me first. I'll call you when I think he's ready."

Anger flared in his eyes. Mac opened his mouth to say something, clamped it shut and nodded curtly instead.

"Good. I'm glad we understand each other. From what I remember he can be quite a handful. I'm sure it hasn't been easy for you these past few months."

"Actually Johnny has been great. We've enjoyed his company," Mac said, his voice strained as though it would crack any moment. He snatched up the two pieces of luggage while he gathered his composure.

In the foyer Johnny had his face pressed up against Frisky's wiggling body. He didn't look at Mac or Tess when they came out of the den. He didn't look at anyone. Tess's heart broke, anguish compressing her chest.

Dear Heavenly Father, please give us the strength to get through this. Be with Johnny in his new home and help him to adjust to his new situation. He cannot do this alone. He needs

You. Saying the silent prayer gave Tess comfort in the midst of the turmoil that swirled about her. She did draw strength from the words and the knowledge that God was with them, especially Johnny in his time of need.

"Well, we must be going," Mrs. Hocks announced, withdrawing her keys from her purse.

Tears crowded Johnny's eyes. When he blinked several times, one lone tear fell. He sniffed and turned away from the group, his shoulders hunched, his head bowed as he clutched his puppy.

The constriction in Tess's chest expanded. She sucked in a deep breath to ease the tightness. Making her way to the small boy huddled in front of the door, so lost and alone-looking, she took him and Frisky into her embrace and kissed his cheek. She half expected him to say yuck and pull away. He didn't. He drew closer to her as though her nearness could give him the strength he needed to walk out the door.

"Remember, the Lord is with you. You aren't alone," Tess whispered.

He nodded once and finally pulled back, still clasping Frisky as though the puppy were his lifeline.

Tess moved to the side and allowed Amy,

Nina and Mac to say their goodbyes. Amy cried, throwing her arms around Johnny and refusing to let go. Mac gently pried her loose and gestured for Nina to hold her while Mac turned to Johnny.

"It has been such a pleasure to have you in my house." Mac glanced at Johnny's aunt and added, "You're always welcome here." He hugged the boy, then backed away, his eyes glistening with unshed tears.

Tess took Mac's hand while Mrs. Hocks opened the door and Johnny and his aunt left. The click of the lock sounded in the deadly quiet and seemed to echo through the spacious foyer, announcing Johnny's departure as final. Amy's sobs cut into the silence and propelled Mac into action. He took his daughter into his arms and held her tightly against him, her cheek pressed against his chest, his chin resting on top of her head.

"Baby, we will see Johnny again. I know that in here." Mac touched the place over his heart. "God didn't bring him into our lives only to take him away."

"I don't know about you, Amy, but I could use a large glass of milk and some of the chocolate chip cookies I baked this afternoon." Nina stroked the child's back.

Lifting her head, Amy sniffled.

"Cookies? Chocolate chip?"

"Your favorite. Ready to help me devour a whole plate of them?"

"I won't ruin my dinner?"

"Since when has that concerned you, young lady? Come on."

When Mac set Amy on the floor, she took Nina's hand and headed with the housekeeper toward the kitchen. Mac stared at the departing pair, his gaze clouded, a frown on his face.

"I'm calling Johnny. I don't care what his aunt said. I can't let that child think I've abandoned him. He's had enough of that in his short life." Mac flexed his hands, then curled them slowly.

Tess wrapped her fingers around one fist and brought it up between them. "Let Mrs. Hocks know you would like to adopt Johnny."

"Oh, I intend to first thing tomorrow morning. Dottie Brown may be Johnny's aunt, but we are more his family than she." He relaxed his grip, brushing one finger across her cheek. "Pray with me, Tess. I need all the help I can get."

"Of course."

Mac bowed his head. "Heavenly Father, I need Your guidance and help. I want Johnny to be a part of my family. Show me the way. In Christ's name, amen."

The simple prayer washed over Tess, renewing her faith in the Lord and easing any tension she felt with Johnny's departure. The Lord had brought Johnny and Mac together. Everything would work out for the best.

The insistent ringing pulled Tess toward wakefulness. She fumbled for the phone and brought the receiver to her ear. "Hello." She squinted at the digital clock and saw it was three o'clock in the morning. News in the middle of the night was never good.

"Tess, Mac here."

The haze clouding her mind evaporated, and she struggled to a sitting position. "What's wrong?" Her heart began to thump against her rib cage.

"Dottie Brown called and told me that Johnny is gone from the hotel room. She got up in the middle of the night and noticed his bed was empty. No one in the hotel saw him leave."

"Has she called the police?"

"Yes. She wanted to know if Johnny was at my house."

Tess heard the anger in Mac's voice and could imagine the grip he had on the phone.

It would match hers. "What are you not telling me?"

"She all but accused me of kidnapping the boy. Nina and I looked, and he isn't here. Will you help me search for him?"

"I would have been upset if you hadn't asked me."

"I'll pick you up in twenty minutes. We'll check his usual haunts first. I have to do something. I can't sit and wait for the police to call."

"I understand. I seem to remember you keeping me company one night while I searched."

"I thought we'd gotten beyond this."

"A lot has happened to Johnny in the past few days. Running away is his usual way of coping. I should have figured something like this would happen."

"Be there in a while. Thanks."

Tess hung up, Mac's desperation and appreciation still sounding in her mind. She quickly switched on the lamp by her bed and got dressed in a pair of old jeans and a sweatshirt. It would be a long night, and comfort would be important.

So as not to awaken Delise, Tess waited outside her apartment for Mac to pick her up in his car. The second he turned into the parking lot, she hurried toward him, not wanting to waste a minute of their search time.

Inside she buckled up, saying, "Let's start in the warehouse district."

Before he backed out of the parking space, he gripped her hand, his gaze on her. "I should have said something tonight when Dottie Brown came. Johnny's run away because he thinks no one really wants him. After meeting the woman, I knew her heart wasn't in this. She told me tonight she was only taking Johnny in because of her duty to her brother. Johnny's a smart kid. He would have picked up on those vibes."

"Well, when we find him you'll have a chance to make it up to him and tell him you want to adopt him."

"If we find him."

Her grasp tightened on his hand. "We will. God brought you two together because He wanted you to be a family. Believe that." She heard him release a rush of air. "Johnny's in good hands."

The tension in his body relaxed. "You're right. The Lord is watching out for him. He'll be all right until we find him."

Tess eased back in the seat, calmness descending. Her faith would sustain her through the search and help her be there for Mac.

"I want to be here when Amy wakes up, then we'll go back out looking for Johnny," Mac said as he let himself into his house, the bright light of dawn slanting across the front lawn.

Tess followed him to the kitchen. "I know he's okay."

"How?" Mac asked wearily, tossing his keys onto the counter by the coffeemaker.

"I just do. I can't explain it."

"I'm so tired, I could drink a whole pot of coffee and still fall asleep." Mac measured out several scoops and dumped them into the top of the small appliance. "These past few nights I haven't slept very well."

"Why don't you go lay down for a while? I'll let you know when Amy gets up." Tess took over the job of making the coffee and waved him out of the kitchen.

A yelp from the utility room caught Mac's attention. "I'll let Buttons out. She's getting pretty good about going to the bathroom in the back yard. She and Frisky were quite a pair." Mac's voice tightened around the last few words.

"Don't worry about her. I'll let her in when she wants in."

Mac picked up Buttons and strolled to the door. He placed the puppy on the deck, then watched as she bounded across the wooden planks, coming to a screeching halt at the chaise lounge. Mac started to close the door, then took a good look at the chair. Buttons's barking filled the air.

"Tess!" Mac called as he raced for the bundle curled in a ball on the chaise lounge. Frisky poked her head up through the middle of the pile and answered Buttons's greeting.

Tess rushed out the back door just as Johnny stretched and sat up, rubbing the sleep from his eyes. Frisky leaped down and began to play tag with Buttons.

Mac drew the boy into his arms. "How long have you been here?"

Johnny looked around him and smiled at Tess. "A while. I didn't want to wake you guys up."

"I've been up most of the night searching for you."

The gruff sound to Mac's voice made Johnny frown and pull back. "I didn't mean to cause no trouble." His lower lip quivered, and he bit it.

"Trouble? Your aunt thinks I kidnapped you."

"I can leave." With his eyes unusually bright, Johnny chewed on his lower lip, not making a move to leave.

"No way." Mac hugged the child to him. "You're part of my family, and I'm gonna fight to keep you this time."

"You mean that?" Johnny said through the tears streaming down his face.

The thickness in Tess's throat grew. Her tears fell. She pressed her hand on Johnny's back and said, "He means it. I can't begin to tell you how frantic Mac and I were last night looking for you."

Leaning back, Johnny stared at Mac. "Then why did you let me go yesterday with that lady?"

"She's your aunt. I thought you would want to be with your own family."

"I don't know her. She didn't want to keep Frisky. She kept sneezing and looking strangely at Frisky. She had the hotel put her in a dog kennel out back. Frisky didn't like it. I had to rescue her."

"Then you wouldn't mind me adopting you?"

"Really? You want me?"

"Yes, very much." Mac grinned. "I'll even take Frisky."

Johnny threw his arms around Mac. "You won't be able to give me back?"

"No, this will be for keeps."

Tess's smile matched Mac's and Johnny's. Her heart swelled with emotions she had cautiously allowed back into her life. Family, children were so important. She wanted it all, a loving husband, a house full of children.

"I'll be the best son you ever had."

Mac grew serious. "I want you to come to me if you're upset. Running away won't solve your problems. I will love you no matter what, and we can work through anything. Just don't run away again."

Johnny's expression equaled Mac's in gravity. "I promise I won't."

"Thanks. I think I lost five years tonight searching for you. I'm not as young as I used to be." Mac tousled Johnny's hair.

The back door banged open, and Amy raced outside, launching herself at Johnny. Mac caught her before she managed to topple Johnny onto the decking.

"You're back. I just knew you would be. I prayed real hard last night, and God heard me."

Mac cradled both children. "How would you feel if Johnny was a member of our family? Would you like a big brother?"

Amy's eyes grew round. "You mean it, Daddy?"

"Yep."

Amy jumped up and down, clapping her hands. "We're gonna be a family. We're gonna be a family."

Sadness intertwined with Tess's happiness as she watched the three of them bond. She took a step away from them, feeling as though she was intruding on them.

Mac glanced up and caught her backing away. "Where do you think you're going?"

She shrugged, not wanting to explain the feelings bombarding her. "I was gonna check on the coffee. Didn't you say you wanted a whole pot of it?"

"I'm wide awake now. I couldn't sleep if I wanted to. Let's get Nina and all of us go out for a big breakfast."

"Yes," the two children yelled and raced for the door.

Mac hung back, grabbing Tess before she followed the children into the house. "After I give Mrs. Hocks and Dottie Brown a call to tell them about Johnny, we're all going to breakfast, including you, then you and I are gonna talk. It's long overdue."

Johnny and Amy hit the house and sprinted for the utility room to get their puppies and go out back to play. Nina shook her head and trailed the children into the kitchen.

"I'm exhausted just looking at those two," Mac said, starting to toss his keys on the table in the foyer.

Tess stifled a yawn, feeling the exhaustion of a long night searching for Johnny and a morning spent celebrating his safe return to the MacPhersons.

Mac peered at her and closed his hand around his keys. "Come on. I'll take you home."

"What about our talk?" Tess wasn't sure she would be able to put two coherent sentences together.

"We'll talk on the way."

On the ride to her apartment Tess rested her head on the seat and listened to the classical music Mac popped into his CD player. Her eyelids began to droop as the sounds of Bach filled the car with soothing tones. The next thing she realized Mac was gently shaking her awake. Her eyes opened and her gaze connected with his. The tenderness in his expression quickened her heartbeat.

She sat up, smoothing her hair. "I'm sorry. I know you wanted to talk, but I couldn't keep my eyes open."

"I hated to wake you up. You looked so serene. Like an angel."

The huskiness in his voice prodded her heart to beat even faster. "That's exactly what I thought Amy looked like the other night when I put her to bed."

"Yeah, she has her moments."

"She's wonderful. You're lucky."

"Yes, I am. It's been a while since I've thought that. You've made me realize that."

"How?" The question came out in a breathless rush.

"After Sheila died, I thought that part of my life was over. With you, Tess, I see it doesn't have to be." He raked his fingers through his hair and massaged the back of his neck. "I'm not doing a very good job of saying what I mean. I hadn't meant to say anything, since you were so tired. I was gonna wait till later." He clasped her hands, bringing her around to face him. "But here goes. Tess Morgan, I love you and want to marry you."

Her world exploded into bright lights and beautiful music. She felt like dancing and singing, all weariness slipping away. "Marry you?"

"Yes. Will you?"

Emotions she'd thought denied to her since Kevin's death tugged at her heart. She had to swallow several times before she could answer, "Yes. Yes, I would love to marry you."

Mac dragged her to him and settled his mouth over hers. Her heart soared, her pulse racing with elation. When he leaned back, the smile that graced his lips sent a warm tingling to the tips of her toes.

"This isn't how I had planned to propose to you, Tess. You deserve flowers, a candle-light dinner and soft music. After all that's happened I couldn't wait for the perfect moment."

She framed his face with her hands. "This was perfect. You've made me the happiest woman alive. For years I've dreamed of marrying the man I love and having a family, the bigger the better."

His jaw tensed beneath her fingertips. A rush of air was expelled from his lips. "Amy and Johnny need a mother."

"Not just Amy and Johnny." Tess saw a frown carve deep lines into his face. "I know you have reservations about having more children, but —"

He jerked away, his body flattened against the driver's door. "I don't want any more children. I told you about my wife when we went camping in the mountains. Amy and Johnny are enough for me. My family is complete."

The steel thread in his voice underscored his words with a clarity that alarmed Tess. Because he was such a good father, she had never believed he wouldn't want to be a father again and again. The dream that had materialized in her mind vanished like a mirage in a desert. "Yes, you told me about Sheila dying during childbirth, but —"

"I will never be responsible for another death. I couldn't take that. It nearly killed me when Sheila died. I won't risk that kind of loss again."

"But you weren't responsible." She frowned, her exhaustion returning tenfold.

"She wouldn't have been pregnant if I hadn't talked her into it. She wouldn't have died giving birth if I hadn't persuaded her that we were ready for a family. You see, I wanted a large one. She wasn't sure she wanted any children. It was probably the one bone of contention in our marriage."

Dread wove its way through her body, making her limbs leaden. "But I want children. We agree on that."

"No, we don't. I've changed my mind."

The air in the car was stifling as though the last breath was being squeezed from it. Tess yanked on the handle and pushed the door open. She quickly stood and wished she hadn't. The world tilted and spun with her sudden movement. She gripped the car and closed her eyes, willing the spinning to stop.

She heard Mac slam his door. When she opened her eyes, he blocked her path, anguish in his features.

"I don't think I can do it, Tess."

"It isn't common for a woman to die in childbirth. I'm willing to take the risk."

"I'm not."

"Weren't you the one who once told me that life is a risk?"

"I've changed my mind where you're concerned."

Again that steel thread ran through his voice, and Tess was reminded of an immovable force. "I don't know what to say. I need to think."

"Do that. I want us to agree if we do get married. I won't go into a marriage again without that settled up front."

This should be the happiest day of her life, but instead she felt deflated, unsure what to do. She loved Mac. But she wanted children badly. Yes, Amy and Johnny would be a part of her family if she married Mac, but she wanted to experience having children, holding and nursing a baby. She was afraid she would always feel incomplete if she gave in on this.

"But you need to think, too, Mac. Life is a risk, and you changing your mind won't alter that fact. Some things are important enough that you should take a risk. This is one of them."

"What if I don't feel that way?"

"Then we have a lot of thinking and talking to do before anything can be decided." She stepped around him, needing to escape to do that thinking. When she was with Mac, she wanted to give in to him, and yet she was afraid that would be the worst mistake of her life. One day she would resent giving up her dream of having children. "I'd better go inside. It's been a long night, and I'm very tired."

As she passed him, he grabbed her arm and held her still. He leaned into her, his face buried in her hair. He kissed the top of her head, then lifted her chin to caress her lips with his.

"I can't change how I feel, Tess."

"Yes, you can."

"But so can you."

"I see we're at opposite ends on this issue. Good day, Mac. I'll talk to you tomorrow."

"Promise?" He released her, a troubled look in his eyes.

"Of course. I agree we have to talk this out before we decide on getting married. I'm working tomorrow, but we can see each other in the evening."

The long walk to her apartment felt as though it took an eternity. She sensed Mac watching her until she disappeared inside and collapsed against the door. Sliding to the floor, she curled her legs up and rested her forehead on her knees. She should be dancing and singing. Instead, she wanted to crawl into bed and bury herself under tons of blankets.

Please, God, help me decide what is best for me, for Mac. I can't do this without You.

Chapter Thirteen

Exhaustion clung to Tess like cobwebs to a deserted house. She stared at the computer monitor at the nurses' station, the words about a new admission blurring. She rubbed her hands down her face to clear her thoughts. All night she'd tossed and turned, trying to come to a decision concerning Mac. Still the answer evaded her. Could she make a commitment to Mac knowing she would give up a lifelong dream?

"Tess, there's a call for you," the unit secretary said.

Tess glanced up from the computer, her brow furrowed.

"Line two."

Tess picked up the phone. "Tess Morgan."

"This is Joan in emergency. I think you should get down here. Peter MacPherson was just brought in. He's been in some kind of accident or something. I don't know the details."

For a few seconds Tess's mind went blank. Her nerveless fingers dropped the receiver, and the sound of it hitting the counter resonated through the nurses' station, jerking her out of her trance.

She quickly snatched up the phone and said, "Is he —"

"He's lost a lot of blood. I don't know much beyond that."

"I'll be there."

Tess placed the phone in its cradle and leaped to her feet. She frantically scanned the area for the head nurse. When she saw Kathleen, she hurried to her and explained about the emergency, a sense of urgency taking hold.

She hadn't been able to say goodbye to Kevin. What if Mac — *Oh, Lord, please watch over Mac. Please don't take him from me.*

Two minutes later she was on the elevator, counting the floors as it descended. Her heartbeat picked up speed as she came nearer. By the time the doors swished open and she rushed out, maneuvering her way among people waiting to get on, her pulse hammered against her temples as though a kettledrum was inside her head.

Joan was waiting for her and pointed to Room Three. Tess shoved through the door and came to a halt just inside. Mac lay on a gurney with two nurses and a doctor hovering over him. Never before had the sight of blood made her light-headed. But seeing Mac helpless with his eyes closed and his face pale while the emergency room team worked on him caused her head to spin. Smells she should be used to assailed her, prompting her stomach to roil. She gripped the edge of the counter to keep from collapsing while trying not to hyperventilate.

"Tess, what are you doing here?" the doctor asked.

"He's a friend. What happened?"

"A gunshot wound to the left shoulder."

"Gunshot?" She didn't understand how something like this could happen to her Mac. He hated guns. He didn't have any in his house.

The doctor returned his attention to his patient. "You don't look too good. Why don't you sit in the waiting area? As soon as I have some information, I'll let you know. You might want to contact his family."

Part of her wanted to stay, try to help, but another part needed to leave the room before she fainted, something she had never done in her whole life. In the corridor she drew in deep breaths of the antiseptic-scented air. Normally the smell didn't bother her. Right now it made her stomach churn, and she fought the urge to throw up.

Visions of Kevin lying in his own blood, his life forces draining away while she held him cradled to her, hounded her all the way down the hall to the waiting area. People milled about, waiting on friends and loved ones. She joined them, crumpling into a chair where she could keep an eye on the door to Room Three.

She knew she needed to tell Mac's family, but she couldn't bring herself to get up and make that call. She didn't know what to say to them. She was afraid she would break down and cry, scaring them more than was necessary. As she twisted her hands together, she prayed as she had never prayed before.

Dear Lord, please don't take Mac away. He's a good man with two children who depend on him. Please be with him and watch over him. Two years before, she had whispered similar words concerning Kevin, and he had died. *Please, it can't happen a second time.*

Unable to sit still, Tess bolted to her feet, her breathing so rapid that the room tilted. She paused, willing herself to take calming breaths before she headed toward the nurses' station. She needed answers. She needed to do something before she went crazy, worrying and wondering if her past would repeat itself.

As Tess grabbed the phone to call Mac's mother, Justin arrived with Alice next to him. Justin headed for the nurse at the counter while Mac's mother strode to Tess. Alice gripped Tess's hands, her lips compressed in a worried expression.

"Are you all right, my dear?" Alice asked.

Her concern touched Tess. "Are you?"

"My son is in God's hands now."

Tess wished she had the self-assurance Alice did, but all she could think about was how Kevin had died and that history could repeat itself. "I was just about to call you. How did you find out so quickly?"

"Someone at the halfway house called me. Then I talked with a policeman. All I know about what happened is what he told me."

"Who did this to Mac?"

"Some man named Harry got upset and began waving a gun around. Mac tried to talk him into giving it to him."

All color drained from Tess's face. She thought of the scene a few weeks before at the halfway house when Harry had gotten upset. She could easily imagine what had happened an hour ago. The man was like a powder keg, only needing a spark to explode.

"Do Amy and Johnny know?" Tess asked, needing to focus on something other than her imagination.

"Not yet. I wanted to see Mac first. I only called Justin to bring me to the hospital. I was afraid to drive."

"I'd like to go with you when you tell the children."

"Sure." Alice sandwiched Tess's hand between hers. "He will be all right. I know it."

"Do you know he asked me to marry him yesterday?"

"That's great. I was praying he would."

"I haven't told him my answer yet." Tess cast a glance at the door down the hall, wondering what was going on in the room and yet not daring to find out. What if — She didn't want to think about what if. It only sent alarm streaking through her, making her realize how little control she had.

"I know it's a big step."

"Mac doesn't want any more children. I want children," Tess blurted, surprised she was telling Mac's mother the reason they weren't engaged.

Alice shook her head. "He still feels guilty about Sheila." She patted Tess's hand. "Give him time. He'll come around. He adores children and is a wonderful father. It would be a shame if he didn't have any more."

Tess didn't have a chance to reply to Alice. The doctor emerged from Room Three and headed toward them. His expression was neutral, giving nothing away.

"Tess." The doctor nodded toward her. "Is this the man's family?"

"Yes. This is Alice MacPherson, Mac's mother, and this is his brother Justin." Tess shifted to allow Justin to stand next to his mother.

"The bullet went through the upper left shoulder, nicking an artery but just missing the lung. He's weak, but barring any complications he should be fine. We gave him a transfusion and we want to watch him a few days. Rest and time should take care of him."

"When can we see him?"

"They're wheeling him up to surgery now to repair his artery. Once he's settled in his room you can see him." The doctor looked at Mac's mother. "I need some information, Mrs. MacPherson, and to go over a few things with you."

Tess sank back against the counter, feeling as if she had lost a pint of blood, not Mac. He should be okay, but what if an infection took hold and — Hadn't she promised herself not to think about what if? She had to have faith in the Lord to watch out and care for Mac.

Tess stood at the window, watching the sun disappear behind the mountains and the shadows of dusk descend. Like the end of day and the start of night, she felt as though she'd come to a crossroads in her life. She leaned against the wall, her arms over her chest as though to protect her heart. Seeing Mac in a hospital bed churned up all the emotions she'd been desperate to suppress. Dread. Fear. Anger.

Yes, the doctor said he would be fine. But what if this happened again? Mac worked in a halfway house, counseling people who were often distraught, living on the edge. What was to stop some other person from getting upset and taking his frustration out on Mac? All the emotions she'd experienced when Kevin had died flooded her, crushing the breath from her. She sank onto the love seat and doubled over, hugging her arms tightly to her. She couldn't go through that a second time. She didn't have the emotional strength to fight those demons again.

The walls of the room seemed to press closer. She needed to get out before she suffocated from the stale, sterile-smelling air that so reminded her of how close Mac had come to dying. A few inches, and the bullet would have pierced his heart. She surged to her feet and headed for the door.

"Tess."

She froze. She heard Mac try to shift. The sound of his groan forced her to his side. "Don't try to move." She slipped into the chair by his bed, her hand on his arm to still him.

His eyelids fluttered. He licked his lips and swallowed several times. "I'm so thirsty."

Tess, glad to have some mundane task to do, quickly filled a plastic cup with water. Carefully she lifted his head and placed the plastic straw to his mouth, fighting the temptation to hug him to her, to check to make sure nothing else was wrong.

He took a few sips, then smiled, the gesture fading almost instantly. "Thanks. I'm lucky to have my very own private nurse."

The hoarseness in his voice magnified his situation in Tess's mind. Again the need to escape bombarded her. She fought the strong urge, knowing she couldn't leave.

"How do you feel?" she asked, putting the cup on the bedside table.

"Like a herd of wild elephants stomped all over me. Otherwise great."

She stiffened. "Don't!"

"Don't what?"

"Make light of what happened to you. You could have died. An inch or so to the right, and you wouldn't be here. You'd be in the morgue."

"But I'm not. I'm alive, Tess."

She clamped her mouth closed, refusing to say anything, afraid of what she would say if she allowed her emotions free reign.

Mac fumbled for her hand. "Tess?"

Tears stung her eyes. She blinked, and a few coursed down her cheeks. "What happened?"

"Harry didn't like how things were progressing at the halfway house. He wanted me to make some changes. To be honest I don't think he intended to hurt me. I think things just got out of hand for him."

"Are you going back?"

Mac's forehead creased. "Yes, why wouldn't I?" He tried to shift again and winced.

"That's why. Look at what Harry did to you." She tried to keep the worry from her voice, but she knew Mac heard it.

"That was a freak accident."

"You breaking your leg was a freak accident. What Harry did wasn't." The force behind her words surprised her.

Mac sighed, his eyes drifting closed for a moment. "I'm gonna be fine, Tess."

This time, Tess thought, but kept her opinion to herself. "You need to rest."

"Will you stay until I fall asleep?"

He looked so vulnerable lying in a hospital bed with tubes attached to him. It took a great deal of effort to sit next to him and not fall apart at the sight of him. "I won't go anywhere."

His eyes slid closed. "Good. When I wake up, I want to talk about us getting married."

Tess watched his face relax in sleep. Pain contracted her chest as though she had been the one shot. Married. How could they? She wanted children. He didn't. He wanted to continue his work at the halfway house. She didn't want him to. She felt the gulf between them widen. One of the hardest things she would have to do was tell Mac she couldn't marry him. She knew her limits, and today she had hit a wall.

Tess ushered Amy and Johnny into the hospital room. Bright light poured through the window, accentuating the dozen arrangements of flowers Mac had received over the past forty-eight hours.

Propped up in bed, Mac grinned at the children. "It's about time you came to visit.

I've missed you two."

Amy hopped up next to her father and hugged him. "Tess said you'll be coming home tomorrow." Her face screwed into a frown. "Why did that bad man hurt you, Daddy? I don't like him."

"He didn't mean to. He has problems I was trying to help him with. He isn't bad, just hurting and confused."

"I was scared." Amy snuggled close to Mac, sticking her thumb into her mouth.

"Me, too," Johnny mumbled.

"As you two can see, I am fine. There's nothing to be afraid of. I'll always be there for you." Mac looked over his daughter's head and straight into Tess's gaze. "Always."

The door clicked open, and Alice came into the room.

"Mom, I'm glad you're here. I bet these two would love to sample the ice cream sundaes they have downstairs in the cafeteria. I hear they are the best."

"Ice cream!" Amy's eyes widened. "Yes!" She pumped her arm in the air as she had seen Johnny do so many times.

"I can take —" Tess started to say.

"I want to talk with Tess for a moment. You two go with Grandma. I'll see you when you get back."

Amy planted a big kiss on Mac's cheek. Johnny gave him a quick hug, looking somewhat embarrassed by all the emotions being expressed. When the children followed Alice from the room, the silence that descended was thick and heavy. Tess could hear the hammering of her heart in her ears. She avoided looking at Mac for a long moment — just as she'd avoided being alone with him the past two days — but she knew the time for reckoning was at hand.

"Okay, Tess, what gives? You've gone to a great deal of trouble to make sure you're not alone with me these past few days. What are you not telling me?"

"This isn't going to work."

"What?"

The question hung in the air between them for a moment. "I'd rather talk later when you're feeling better."

"So you want me to be in good condition before you dump me."

The accusation cut through the tension that captured Tess and tore at her defenses. "I want children. You don't. I don't see a future for us." She looked away from the anger that sparked in his eyes, wishing their situation were that simple.

"Is that all?"

"Isn't that enough?"

"I think there's more to it than just not agreeing on the number of children we would have."

She bit the inside of her cheek. How could she tell him she would be afraid every day he walked out of the house that something would take him away? "You said yourself you wanted to settle the issue before getting married. Have you changed your mind? Do you want more children?"

His forehead wrinkled in a deep, thoughtful frown. "I don't know. I've been pretty out of it for the past few days."

"You wanted this discussion. I was willing to wait."

"To tell me it was over?"

"I don't see there's anything to discuss. We want two different things in life." She swallowed the lump in her throat, determined now that he had started the conversation to end their relationship so she could start healing. The road to recovery would be long, one she wasn't sure she would ever finish. Her heart ached with wants and needs only Mac could fulfill.

"I want to talk about it some more. I love you, Tess."

Emotions, all wrapped up in her love for this man, swamped her. But she remembered the terror that gripped her when she saw him in the emergency room, his blood everywhere as the nurse tore his shirt away to reveal his wound. "I just can't."

"Can't what?"

Johnny, Amy and Alice entered the room, saving Tess from having to answer. She fled before she broke down in front of the children. She felt the tears flowing down her cheeks. She saw people staring at her as she rushed toward the elevator. Sounds and smells faded from her consciousness. She focused her attention on one thing — finding a sanctuary.

Without realizing it, she ended up in front of the double doors that led into the hospital chapel. She pushed through them and sank onto a pew. Lacing her fingers together, she bowed her head. Her mind went blank for a few seconds, then the words poured into her.

Dear Heavenly Father, I'm lost and don't know what to do. I love Mac so much. What if he had died the other day?

The silence in the chapel amplified the loneliness she felt. What would she have if she walked away from Mac?

Please, God, I need You. I need Your help. What do I do? What do You want from me?

"Tess."

She pivoted in the pew and saw Mac

standing in the doorway. He moved into the chapel, his gaze trained on hers, such tenderness and love in his eyes that her heart screamed out the injustice. The pallor of his features and the slowness of his gait attested to the ordeal he had been through, reminding her why she was afraid to commit.

He sat next to her, one corner of his mouth lifting in a smile. "I knew you would be here."

"How?"

"Because this is where I would have come."

"Oh," she murmured, the single word enhancing their bond more than anything.

"Tell me what is really bothering you. Let me help you."

"What if you had died?"

"But I didn't."

"You're going back to the halfway house when you're better. It could happen again."

"Yes, it could."

Pain stabbed her heart as though a bullet had ripped through her.

"But I could be sitting in my easy chair at home and die. When it's my time to go to the Lord, I will go, not one minute before. In the meanwhile, I can't stop living because I'm afraid of what might be."

"I don't want you to go back to the halfway house."

"Is that what you really want? Do you want me to turn my back on my ministry?"

"No — yes. I don't know."

Mac cupped his hand over hers. "I will if that's what you want."

Confusion reigned in Tess. She wanted to shout no, but the word wouldn't come out. How could she ask him to give up something that was so important to him? His strong faith and ministry were an intricate part of him and one of the reasons she loved him so much.

"Now, about having children?"

Tess twisted and pressed her fingers over his mouth. "I love Amy and Johnny as though they were mine." She paused, her throat clogged with emotions. "A family of four is plenty."

"So, we each give up what we want? You think that's fair? You think that's what God wants?"

"I love you, Mac. I'm not sure how this can work. You're right. I can't ask you to give up the halfway house."

"And I can't ask you to give up your dream of having children."

"It looks like we're at a standstill."

"Then we've come to the right place. Our

Father will show us the way. We just have to open our hearts and listen to Him."

She wanted it to be that simple. Could it?

With her hand still linked to Mac's, Tess bowed her head. She wanted the fear gone. How could that happen when she had lived with it so long? She wanted a family. Could she make the emotional commitment without fear of being hurt?

"Our Father, guide us through this challenge You've laid at our feet. Help us to see Your path and to surrender our fear to You. Help us to put our lives in Your hands."

Mac's prayer held the key. The words weaved their way into her heart, and she felt the tension slip away. If she turned her life totally over to the Lord and trusted in Him completely, then she would no longer experience the terror she'd had on that mountaintop two years before. Wasn't that what true faith was all about?

God is with me every step of the way. I will be all right.

Tess angled her head to peer at Mac. Their gazes touched and she realized he felt the same way. A bond, forged through pain, solidified between them as she rested her cheek against his good shoulder and relished the moment of total peace and surrender.

In order to love God, to love Mac, she had to open herself up and let them in with no reservations, no conditions attached. Mac should continue his work because that was part of the Lord's plan. That was a part of Mac, the man she had fallen in love with.

Mac slipped his arm around her shoulder and she nestled into the curve of his body. "I love you, Tess Morgan. I want you to be the mother of my children. Together we both can let go of our fears. We can put our pasts behind us. You were right about life's risks. I can't stop living my life to the fullest because I'm afraid of what could happen."

"Because we will go to the Lord when our time is here, not one minute sooner."

"Yes, we both have to learn to risk in order to love. Grieving is an important process in life, but it should never take over as we both were letting it do. It should never control us to the point we turn away from what is truly important."

"The essence of our faith."

Mac placed a kiss on the top of Tess's head and cradled her closer. "That, and our ability to love another totally and unconditionally as we love our Father in Heaven."

"I do have one condition to place on you continuing your work at the halfway house."

She looked into his face in time to see him arch a brow. "Oh?"

The smile that graced her lips filled her with such love for the man next to her. "I want to volunteer alongside you. What is important to you is important to me."

"And I suppose you'll want me in the delivery room when our first child is born."

"Of course, holding my hand."

He bent forward and touched his lips to hers. "I'll be there every time."

Epilogue

Johnny raced ahead of the large group emerging from the courthouse. "It's done. It's done. I am official."

Tess paused at the top of the stairs and watched the boy dance. Amy joined him, shouting her joy.

Mac came up behind her and wrapped his arms around her, resting his chin on her shoulder. "Do you think our son is excited?"

"No. What makes you think that?"

"Oh, the silly grin on his face, the fact he's waving the adoption papers around for everyone to see."

Tess turned her head slightly to glance at her husband. "Johnny's now legally a member of the family. He's still in remission with high odds in his favor that it will stay that way. You know this year can't get any better."

"I don't know about that." Mac laid his hand over her rounded stomach. "I'd say in

about three months it will."

Amy ran up the stairs and tugged on her father's pant leg. "Come on. Aunt Casey said we need to hurry. Remember the party? Everyone is waiting."

"What party?" Mac asked, his eyes bright with humor.

Amy twisted her mouth in a frown, her brow wrinkled. "The party to celebrate. I want some ice cream and cake before it's all gone."

Casey stopped next to Tess and Mac. "You know, the cake that says Welcome To The Family, Johnny and Colt."

"The MacPhersons are growing by leaps and bounds," Mac said, noticing Colt take his sister's hand.

Tess smiled at the thought of her family. "And I'm gonna be a beached whale walking down that aisle next month as your matron of honor, Casey."

Mac planted a soft kiss on Tess's cheek. "But a beautiful beached whale."

Dear Readers,

My mother, who passed away recently, was a nurse all her life. I can remember her talking about her work and how much joy she got from being a nurse and helping others during difficult times in their lives. The story of Tess and Mac is a story about giving oneself to others and to God. Faith is what can sustain a person through those difficult times and even strengthen him.

I love hearing from readers. You may write me at P.O. Box 2074, Tulsa, OK, 74101.

May God bless you,

Margaret Daley

About the Author

Margaret Daley feels she has been blessed. She has been married thirty-one years to her husband, Mike, whom she met in college. He is a terrific support and her best friend. They have one son, Shaun, who is marrying his high school sweetheart.

Margaret has been writing for many years and loves to tell a story. When she was a little girl, she would play with her dolls and make up stories about their lives. Now she writes these stories down. She especially enjoys weaving stories about families and how faith in God can sustain a person when things get tough. When she isn't writing, she is fortunate to be a teacher for students with special needs. She has taught for over twenty years and loves working with her students. She has also been a Special Olympics coach and has participated in many sports with her students.

The employees of Thorndike Press hope you have enjoyed this Large Print book. All our Thorndike and Wheeler Large Print titles are designed for easy reading, and all our books are made to last. Other Thorndike Press Large Print books are available at your library, through selected bookstores, or directly from us.

For information about titles, please call:

(800) 223-1244

or visit our Web site at:

www.gale.com/thorndike
www.gale.com/wheeler

To share your comments, please write:

Publisher
Thorndike Press
295 Kennedy Memorial Drive
Waterville, ME   04901